# Claws at the Falls:
## The Cozy Purrch Café Mysteries
### Book 3

## Erica J Whelton

Publisher: Sunseri Design Publishing
ISBN: 978-1-956069-63-1

Printed in the United States of America

To my husband

# Chapter One

The February sun hung low over Larkspur Valley, casting long shadows across Main Street as I unlocked the front door of The Cozy Purrch. Three months had passed since Thanksgiving, since Warren's arrest, since Lily had officially moved to Larkspur Valley and become my partner at the café. The snow still blanketed the mountains, but the days were growing longer, and there was something in the air that whispered of spring.

Inside, the café was warm and quiet. The stone fireplace crackled softly, and the familiar scent of coffee beans and cedar wrapped around me like a welcome home. I flipped on the lights and began my morning routine, a ritual that had become as natural as breathing. The cats followed me down from the apartment, having already eaten their breakfast upstairs.

"I don't see why we have to come down so early," Gus grumbled, settling onto his perch on the cat tree nearest the counter. "The humans won't be here for another hour at least."

"You don't have to come down," I reminded him. "You could stay upstairs."

"And miss judging the customers? Never."

Poppy stretched languidly on her heated bed near the fireplace. "Leave him alone, Alexis. You know how he gets before the caffeine smell kicks in."

Rocky bounded down from somewhere near the ceiling, his orange fur a blur of chaotic energy. "I love mornings! Everything is exciting in the morning! What are we doing? Are we doing things?"

"We're opening the café," I said. "Same as every morning."

"Exciting!"

Millie crept out from behind the fern in the corner, her Siamese markings elegant even as she moved with her characteristic nervousness. "Is it safe? No loud noises this morning?"

"All quiet," I assured her.

Sage, the tiny gray kitten I'd rescued last fall, tumbled down the last few stairs, still not quite coordinated enough for a graceful descent. She was growing fast, her gangly legs finally starting to catch up with her oversized ears, but she was still small enough to fit in my cupped hands, still young enough that everything was an adventure.

"I'm going to explore the whole café today," Sage announced. "Every corner. Even the corners I explored yesterday. And then I'm going to find new corners that nobody has ever discovered before."

"There are no new corners," Gus said. "We've lived here for years. Every corner has been thoroughly documented."

"But what if there are secret corners? Hidden ones?"

"There are no secret corners."

"You don't know that for certain."

Gus sighed the sigh of a cat who had given up on the younger generation. "Just stay out of my way."

I checked on the adoption room, where three other cats were still sleeping in their various beds. Whiskers, an older tabby who'd been with us for two months, opened one eye and promptly closed it again. Not a morning cat. The two younger ones, siblings named Penny and Copper, were curled together in a patch of early sunlight, their ginger and cream fur intertwined so completely it was hard to tell where one ended and the other began.

"Those two will find a home soon," Poppy said, joining me at the glass partition. "I can feel it. Someone's coming for them."

"You've been saying that for weeks."

"And I'll keep saying it until it happens. Some things are worth waiting for."

I started the espresso machine, the familiar hiss and gurgle filling the empty café. Through the window, I could see the first hints of life on Main Street. Jasper Sharpe unlocking his general store across the way, pausing to scatter salt on his icy front steps. A few early risers walking toward Flo's diner for breakfast, their breath making clouds in the cold air. The usual Tuesday morning in Larkspur Valley.

The door chimed at precisely seven o'clock, and Lily walked in, her dark hair dusted with snowflakes, her warm brown eyes bright despite the early hour.

"Good morning," she said, shrugging off her coat. "Cold out there. But I think I saw a robin on my way over."

"Already? It's only February."

"Early spring, maybe." She tied on her apron and joined me behind the counter. "Or a very confused bird."

We worked in comfortable silence for a few minutes, Lily restocking the pastry case with the fresh delivery from Flo's diner while I prepared the specialty drinks board for the day. Three months of working together had given us an easy rhythm, the kind of partnership that didn't need words to function. She knew when I needed help without my asking; I knew when she needed space without her saying.

"Colton stopped by the bookshop yesterday," Lily said casually. Too casually.

I focused very intently on writing "Lavender Dreams" on the chalkboard. "Oh? Were you visiting Maeve?"

"Checking in on her. She's been teaching me some new warding techniques." Lily lowered her voice, even though we were alone. "And yes, Colton happened to come in while I was there. He asked about you. Whether you'd thought any more about dinner."

I had thought about it. That was the problem. I'd thought about it quite a lot, turning the invitation over in my mind like a stone I couldn't quite put down. Colton was kind. Attentive. Handsome in that rugged veterinarian way that made half the single women in town find excuses to bring their pets in for checkups. He'd made his interest clear over the past few months, patient but persistent, and I'd run out of excuses to keep deflecting.

"Maybe I should say yes," I said, not quite believing the words as they left my mouth.

Lily's eyebrows rose. "Really?"

"I've been hiding for so long. Maybe it's time to stop."

"That's a big step." Her voice was gentle, free of judgment. "Opening yourself up to someone new, letting them close. Are you sure you're ready for that?"

Over a year in Larkspur Valley now. Over a year of building a life, making friends, becoming part of a community. Over a year without a single sign that the coven was looking for me, without any hint that they knew where I'd gone. Maybe they'd given up. Maybe two years was long enough for them to stop caring about one runaway witch who'd never wanted their power in the first place.

Or maybe I was fooling myself. But if I spent my whole life waiting for danger that might never come, was that really living at all?

I wasn't sure of anything. But I was tired of being afraid, tired of keeping everyone at arm's length, tired of watching life happen to other people while I stood on the sidelines. For two years I'd been running, hiding, building walls so high I couldn't see over them anymore. Maybe it was time to try something different.

"No," I admitted. "But maybe that's the point. Maybe I'll never feel ready, and I just have to do it anyway."

Before Lily could respond, the door chimed again. Our first customer of the day.

Mabel Smalls shuffled in, sharp eyes sweeping the café with her usual keen observation. At eighty-two, she missed nothing and forgot even less. The town's unofficial historian, she knew every family's secrets going back four generations and had opinions about all of them. She claimed her regular corner table and waited expectantly.

"Lavender Dreams?" I asked, already reaching for her usual cup.

"You know me too well, dear." She settled into her chair with a contented sigh. "Cold morning. Good for staying inside with a warm drink and a puzzle."

I brought her the tea and she wrapped her weathered hands around the cup, breathing in the steam. She already had her crossword book out on the table, pen resting beside it.

"You look thoughtful this morning, Alexis. Something on your mind?"

"Just thinking about the future," I said, which was vague enough to be true.

"The future is overrated. The present is where life happens." She gave me a knowing look over the rim of her cup. "Though I hear Dr. Dover has been asking around about you. Seems quite smitten."

Small towns. Nothing stayed secret for long.

"I hear a lot of things," I said noncommittally.

"I'm sure you do." Mabel smiled and finally opened her crossword book, but there was a twinkle in her eye that suggested this conversation wasn't over, merely postponed.

The morning rush began in earnest around eight. Regulars filed in one after another, seeking their caffeine fixes and a moment of warmth before facing the February chill. I made drinks, exchanged pleasantries, and fell into the comfortable rhythm of running a café.

At eight-fifteen, Sheriff Iris Scott appeared. She ordered her usual black coffee and lingered at the counter, her expression thoughtful.

"Quiet week," she said.

"Is that a complaint?"

"Observation." She took a sip of her coffee. "After last fall, quiet is good. I could use a few more quiet months."

I understood what she meant. Warren's arrest had shaken the town, and the revelation that one of their founding family descendants was a murderer had taken time to process. But Larkspur Valley was resilient. Slowly, steadily, life had returned to normal.

"How's the consultant position working out?" Iris asked. "I know I haven't called on you yet, but I wanted you to know it's still on the table."

"Whenever you need me," I said. And I meant it. The offer she'd extended after Warren's arrest had surprised me, but it had also felt right. A way to use whatever instincts I had for something good.

Iris nodded and headed for her usual table, where she could watch the door and monitor the room without seeming to. Old habits.

The morning continued in its steady flow. Cordelia from the yarn shop stopped in for her usual chamomile, chattering about the new shipment of merino wool she was expecting. Jasper crossed the street for his mid-morning dark roast, grumbling about the weather and the tourists who couldn't handle a little snow. Esther, the high school English teacher, picked up her standing order of three lattes for herself and her colleagues, already looking harried despite the early hour.

At nine o'clock, the bell chimed and my heart did something complicated. Lionel walked in, strawberry blond hair tousled from the wind, green eyes crinkling with his easy smile. He was carrying a book tucked under one arm, which wasn't unusual. What was unusual was that he set it on the counter as he approached.

"Morning, Alexis." He slid onto one of the counter stools with that comfortable familiarity he'd always had, like he belonged wherever he happened to be. "The usual, when you get a chance."

I reached for the dandelion root blend I kept specifically for him. "Coming right up."

"Oh, and this is for you." He nudged the book toward me. "Found it at an estate sale last weekend. Made me think of you."

I picked it up, examining the worn cover. It was a vintage mystery novel, the kind with a beautifully illustrated dust jacket showing a woman in silhouette against a moonlit window. The title read "The Cat Who Knew Too Much."

"Lionel, this is gorgeous." I opened it carefully, noting the gilt-edged pages and the inscription on the title page: "To Mildred, who always believes in happy endings. With love, 1952."

"It's a first edition. Not valuable or anything, but the illustrations are wonderful." He shrugged, as if giving someone a thoughtfully chosen vintage book was nothing special. "I know you like mysteries. And cats. Seemed like a perfect fit."

"It is. Thank you."

"Sure." He smiled, and that was it. No expectation of anything in return, no lingering to see my reaction, no making a production of the gesture. He simply accepted his tea when I handed it over and asked, "How's Sage settling in? Last time I was here, she was trying to climb the curtains."

"She's graduated to exploring every corner of the café. Twice daily, minimum."

"Thorough. I respect that." He glanced toward the cat tree, where Sage was indeed investigating the space behind it with great intensity. "She's gotten so big since October. Still has those ridiculous ears, though."

"She'll grow into them eventually. Probably."

"I don't know. I kind of hope she doesn't. They give her character."

He took his tea to a corner table near the window and pulled out his phone, settling in to work. Within minutes he was absorbed in whatever he was doing, occasionally glancing up to smile at passing customers or watch the snow falling outside. He didn't look at me, didn't seem to need anything from me. Just existed in the same space, comfortable and content.

"I like that one," Poppy observed quietly from her perch.

"I know you do."

"He brought you a present. About cats."

"It's just a book."

"It's never just a book. Books are important." She licked her paw thoughtfully. "He remembered about the kitten. Asked about her by name."

"He has a good memory."

"He pays attention. There's a difference."

Before I could respond, the door chimed again, and a familiar figure walked in.

Grant Granger had become a regular over the past two weeks. Tall, mid-forties, with graying temples and the kind of tan that spoke of time spent outdoors. He always carried a laptop, always claimed the same table by the window, always ordered the same drink: a simple black coffee with an extra shot of espresso.

"Morning, Grant," I called out. "The usual?"

"Please." He settled into his chair and opened his laptop immediately, fingers flying over the keys. "Any chance you have those scones from Flo's? The blueberry ones?"

"Just got a fresh batch this morning."

"Perfect. I'll take two."

I prepared his order and brought it to his table. Up close, I could see the tension in his shoulders, the way his eyes kept flicking to the window like he was watching for something. Or someone.

"Working on the book?" I asked, nodding toward his laptop.

He'd told me about it when he first started coming in. A travel book about hidden mountain towns, the secret gems that tourists overlooked. Larkspur Valley, he claimed, was exactly the kind of place he was looking for.

"Research today," he said, and there was something tight in his voice. "Trying to nail down some details about the local hiking trails. The falls in particular."

"Aspen Falls? It's beautiful this time of year. Partially frozen, but stunning."

"That's what I've heard." He took a sip of his coffee, and I noticed his hand trembling slightly. "Do you know anyone who could show me around? I'd hate to get lost out there."

"Atticus Monroe is the park ranger. He knows those trails better than anyone. He comes in most mornings around ten."

"I'll keep an eye out. Thanks, Alexis."

I left him to his work, but something nagged at me as I returned to the counter. Grant had been coming in for over two weeks, but I still couldn't get a read on him. He was friendly enough, asked lots of questions about the area, tipped well. But there was something beneath the surface. A nervousness that didn't quite fit with his casual demeanor.

"He smells like secrets," Gus observed from his perch. He'd finished his post-breakfast nap and was now engaged in his favorite mid-morning activity: judging the customers.

"Everyone has secrets," I reminded him.

"His are bigger than most."

Poppy joined him on the cat tree, her calico fur gleaming in the morning light. "He's not dangerous," she said thoughtfully. "Nervous, yes. Scared, maybe. But not dangerous."

"Scared of what?" I asked.

"That's the question, isn't it?"

The morning continued. More customers came and went. Lily and I worked in our comfortable rhythm, exchanging smiles and small talk and the occasional observation about the weather or the customers.

At ten o'clock, as promised, Atticus Monroe walked through the door.

The park ranger was a quiet man, more comfortable with animals than people. He had an easy way of moving, unhurried and deliberate, like someone who spent most of his time in the wilderness and had learned to match its pace. His dark hair was starting to gray at the temples, and his weathered face spoke of decades spent outdoors.

"Morning, Atticus. The usual?"

"Please." He took his regular seat at the counter, nodding politely to the other customers. "Cold out there today. Saw some interesting tracks near the falls this morning."

"What kind of interesting?"

"Mountain lion. Big one, judging by the prints." He accepted his black coffee with a grateful nod. "She's been hanging around that area for a few weeks now. Probably has a den nearby."

"Should people be worried?"

"Just aware. Keep their distance, don't approach any wildlife. The usual." He took a sip of his coffee, and something flickered across his face. A frown, quickly suppressed. "There's been some strange activity out there lately."

"Strange how?"

"The animals are skittish. More than usual for this time of year. Like something's got them spooked." He shook his head. "Probably nothing. Could just be the weather patterns."

But I knew Atticus well enough by now to recognize when he wasn't saying everything. There was something about the way he held himself, tense despite his relaxed posture, that suggested he was troubled.

From his table by the window, Grant Granger was watching us. Listening. When I caught his eye, he looked away quickly, returning his attention to his laptop.

"That the travel writer?" Atticus asked, following my gaze.

"Grant Granger. He's working on a book about mountain towns. He was actually asking about a guide earlier. Wants to know more about the hiking trails, especially around Aspen Falls."

Atticus studied Grant with the same keen observation he probably used to track wildlife. "He should be careful out there. The falls can be dangerous this time of year. Ice makes the trails slippery, and the water's cold enough to kill you in minutes if you fall in."

"I'll make sure to tell him. Actually, he specifically asked if I knew anyone who could show him around. I mentioned you."

Atticus nodded slowly. "I can talk to him. Point out the safe routes, at least."

Before I could say anything else, Grant appeared at the counter. He must have noticed Atticus come in, must have been waiting for exactly this moment.

"Excuse me," he said, and there was an eagerness in his voice that bordered on desperation. "I couldn't help but overhear. You're Atticus Monroe? The park ranger?"

"That's right." Atticus turned on his stool, sizing Grant up with that steady gaze.

"Grant Granger. I'm writing a book about hidden mountain towns." He stuck out his hand, and Atticus shook it after a moment's hesitation. "Alexis mentioned you know the trails around Aspen Falls better than anyone. I was hoping you might be able to help me with some research."

"What kind of research?"

"The falls themselves, mostly. I've heard there are some caves nearby? And some interesting rock formations along the northern trail?"

Something flickered in Atticus's expression. Surprise, maybe, or suspicion. "That's pretty specific knowledge for a travel book."

Grant's smile faltered for just a second before he recovered. "I like to be thorough. Details are what make a book come alive, you know? I don't want to just describe the falls as 'pretty.' I want to capture everything about them."

Atticus took a long sip of his coffee. "The caves aren't on any official trail. Most tourists don't even know they exist."

"That's exactly why I want to see them. The hidden gems, the places only locals know about." Grant leaned forward, and I could see his hands were trembling slightly against his laptop bag. "I'd pay you for your time, of course. A guide fee."

"I don't need money." Atticus set down his cup. "But I could show you around tomorrow, if the weather holds. Meet me at the trailhead at eight. Wear proper boots and bring plenty of water. It's a three-hour hike, minimum."

"That's wonderful. Thank you." Grant's relief was palpable, almost too intense for a simple hiking arrangement. "I really appreciate it, Mr. Monroe."

"Atticus. And don't thank me yet. Those trails are no joke this time of year." He gave Grant one more measuring look. "You sure you're just writing a travel book?"

Grant's expression went carefully blank. "What else would I be doing?"

"No idea. Just asking."

An uncomfortable silence stretched between them. Then Grant nodded stiffly, gathered his laptop bag, and headed back to his table. But he didn't open his laptop. He just sat there, staring out the window, drumming his fingers against the tabletop.

Atticus turned back to me, his voice low. "That one's hiding something."

"I got the same feeling. He's been jumpy ever since he started coming in."

"Jumpy people make mistakes on mountain trails." He finished his coffee and set down some bills. "I'll keep an eye on him tomorrow. See what he's really after."

"Be careful."

"Always am."

The morning wore on. Grant eventually packed up his laptop and left, promising to return tomorrow. Atticus had already headed back to the trails. Lionel lingered over his drink, working contentedly on his phone, occasionally glancing up to watch the snow falling or to smile at a passing customer. He caught my eye once, gave me a small wave, and returned to his work without expectation.

Around eleven, I noticed a man standing outside on the sidewalk.

He wasn't doing anything suspicious, exactly. Just standing there in a heavy coat, looking at his phone. But something about him made me pause. The way he kept glancing at the café between texts. The tension in his shoulders. The way he seemed to be waiting for something.

"That man outside," I murmured to Lily. "Have you seen him before?"

She glanced through the window. "I don't think so. Tourist, maybe?"

"Maybe."

But tourists usually came in. They didn't stand outside in the cold, watching.

The cats had noticed too. Rocky had stopped his endless bouncing and was staring at the window, his orange fur bristled slightly. Even Millie had crept out from behind her fern, her blue eyes fixed on the figure outside.

"Something's wrong with that one," Gus said quietly. "He smells like waiting. Like hunting."

"What do you mean?"

"I don't know exactly. Just... be careful."

Before I could respond, the man put his phone away and walked on, disappearing down Main Street without looking back. I watched him go, filing his unremarkable face away in my memory.

Medium height, medium build, brown hair going gray. The kind of person you'd forget five minutes after meeting them.

"Strange," Lily said.

"Very."

But there was no time to dwell on it. The late morning rush was picking up, and I had drinks to make.

Around noon, when the lunch crowd was dying down, Colton Dover walked in.

The veterinarian was in his civilian clothes today, jeans and a flannel shirt that made him look more like a rugged outdoorsman than a doctor. His hazel eyes found me immediately, and his whole face lit up when he smiled. That was the thing about Colton. When he looked at you, he really looked at you, like you were the only person in the room worth seeing.

"Alexis." He approached the counter with an easy confidence, leaning against it like he belonged there. "I was hoping I'd catch you."

"What can I get you?"

"Just a coffee." But he didn't look at the menu, didn't glance at the specialty board. His attention was entirely on me. "I was wondering if you'd thought any more about dinner. There's a new Italian place in Silverpine. I've heard the chicken piccata is incredible."

This was the moment. The one I'd been avoiding for months. The one Lily and I had just discussed this morning.

Maybe it's time to stop hiding, I'd said.

I looked at Colton. Really looked at him. He was handsome in an uncomplicated way, with kind eyes and an easy smile. He'd been patient with me, never pushing too hard, never making me feel pressured. He'd asked me out three times over the past few months, and each time I'd deflected with excuses about being busy or not being ready. And each time, he'd simply nodded, said he understood, and kept coming back.

That kind of persistence could be annoying. But from Colton, it felt more like steadfastness. Like he'd decided I was worth waiting for and wasn't going to change his mind.

"Okay," I heard myself say. "Let's do it."

Colton's face broke into a grin so genuine it made something warm bloom in my chest. "Really? That's wonderful." He reached across the counter and squeezed my hand briefly, his palm warm against my fingers. "How about tomorrow night? I could pick you up at seven."

"Tomorrow night works. Seven is good."

"I'll make reservations. You're going to love this place, Alexis. They make their pasta fresh daily, and the tiramisu is supposed to be the best in the county." He was already planning, already thinking ahead, his enthusiasm infectious. "Should I pick you up here or at your apartment?"

"Here is fine."

"Perfect. I'll be here at seven sharp." He took his coffee with that same bright smile, looking like I'd just given him the best gift of his life. "I've been looking forward to this for a long time. I promise you won't regret it."

After he left, Lily appeared at my elbow. "So you're really doing this."

"I'm really doing this."

"How do you feel?"

I considered the question carefully. How did I feel? Nervous, certainly. Apprehensive. But also something else. Something that might have been hope, if I squinted at it the right way. Colton was a good man. Everyone said so. He was kind to animals, respected in the community, the sort of person who brought soup to sick neighbors and helped elderly ladies carry their groceries. The kind of man any sensible woman would be lucky to date.

"I feel like I'm finally moving forward," I said. "Whatever that means."

Lily squeezed my arm. "I'm proud of you."

On the cat tree, Poppy was watching me with an expression I couldn't quite read. She didn't say anything, but her tail flicked once, twice, in that contemplative way cats have when they're thinking deep thoughts.

"What?" I asked her.

"Nothing." But she glanced toward the corner table where Lionel had been sitting all morning. He was gone now, must have slipped out while I was talking to Colton. His cup sat empty on the table, and beside it, he'd left a small tip and a napkin with a simple drawing of a cat with enormous ears.

Sage.

He'd drawn Sage.

"Like I said," Poppy murmured. "Nothing at all."

The afternoon passed quietly. Customers came and went. The cats napped in their various spots around the café. Outside, the February sun began its early descent toward the mountains.

At four o'clock, Grant Granger returned.

He was more agitated than this morning, his movements jerky and quick. He ordered another coffee, claimed his usual table, but didn't open his laptop this time. Instead, he sat staring out the window, drumming his fingers on the table.

"Something wrong?" I asked, bringing him his drink.

He startled at my voice, then forced a smile. "Just tired. Preparing for tomorrow's hike."

"The one with Atticus? That should be interesting. He knows those trails better than anyone."

"That's what I'm counting on." Grant wrapped both hands around his coffee cup, as if trying to warm them. "Atticus mentioned some caves near the falls. Places most tourists don't know about."

"Sounds like it'll make great material for your book."

"Yeah. Great material." But his eyes kept flicking to the window, watching the street, watching everyone who passed by.

"You looking for someone?" The question came out before I could stop it.

Grant's expression shuttered. "Just people-watching. Occupational hazard when you write about places. You start studying everyone."

It was a reasonable explanation. But I didn't believe it.

The cats had gathered near my feet, which was unusual. Normally they gave customers space, but all five of them were now clustered near me, watching Grant with identical intensity.

"He's scared," Poppy said softly. "Really scared."

"Of what?" I murmured, low enough that Grant wouldn't hear.

"Something's coming. He knows it. He's been looking over his shoulder for weeks. And I think..." She paused, her tail curling around her paws. "I think it's almost here."

I glanced at Grant, who had returned to his window-watching. Whatever secret he was carrying, it was eating him alive.

But it wasn't my business. Not really. He was just a customer, a tourist passing through on his way to somewhere else. He'd finish his book and move on, and Larkspur Valley would continue as it always had.

I had my own life to worry about. A date to prepare for. A future to tentatively embrace.

Whatever Grant Granger was running from, it had nothing to do with me.

At closing time, he packed up without opening his laptop at all. "See you tomorrow, Alexis. Thanks for the coffee."

"See you tomorrow, Grant."

The door chimed as he left, and I watched him walk down Main Street, hunched against the cold, still looking over his shoulder.

"Something's wrong with that one," Gus observed.

"I know."

"Are you going to do anything about it?"

I thought about it. About the fear in Grant's eyes, the tension in his shoulders, the way he watched every passing stranger like they might be a threat. About the man who'd been standing outside this morning, watching the café with that same nervous energy.

"It's not my problem," I said finally. "He's just a customer."

But even as I said it, I knew I didn't believe it. Something was coming. The cats felt it. Atticus felt it. Even the wildlife near the falls felt it.

And Grant Granger was at the center of whatever it was.

I just didn't know yet that by this time next week, I'd be investigating his murder.

## Chapter Two

Wednesday morning dawned gray and cold, the kind of February day that made you want to stay in bed with a warm blanket and a warmer cat. But cafés don't run themselves, and by six-thirty I was downstairs starting the espresso machine while the cats arranged themselves in their preferred spots.

"It's going to snow," Poppy observed from her window perch. "I can feel it in my whiskers."

"The weather human on the television box said the same thing last night," Rocky added helpfully. "Though I don't trust him. He doesn't have whiskers."

"Nobody trusts weathermen," Gus said. "They're wrong half the time."

"Then why do humans keep listening to them?"

"Because humans aren't very smart about some things."

Sage tumbled off her perch, having attempted to clean her back paw while balancing on the edge. She landed on her feet, of course, and immediately pretended she'd meant to do that.

"I'm practicing my acrobatics," she announced. "For when I need to catch birds."

"You're an indoor cat," Gus reminded her. "You'll never catch a bird."

"I might. You don't know. There could be a bird emergency someday."

"There has never been a bird emergency in the history of this café."

"That just means we're overdue for one."

I left them to their debate and focused on prepping for the morning rush. Lily arrived at seven, shaking snow from her coat.

"It's really starting to come down out there," she said.

"Poppy predicted it earlier." I handed Lily her apron. "She felt it in her whiskers."

Lily smiled. "She's usually right about these things. Better than any weatherman."

"That's what I said!" Rocky called from across the room. "Great minds think alike!"

"Rocky, she can't hear you," I reminded him.

"I know. But it's still nice to be agreed with."

The morning passed in its usual rhythm. Mabel came in for her tea and crossword puzzle, settling into her corner with a contented sigh. Iris stopped by for her black coffee and a brief update on the general state of town peace, which remained peaceful.

"Quiet night," she said. "I'm starting to get suspicious."

"Suspicious of quiet?"

"In my experience, too much quiet usually means something's building." She took a long sip of her coffee. "Probably nothing. Just an old cop's instincts."

Since the snow hadn't started yet, I knew that Grant and Atticus were out on the trails right now. I thought about the fear in his eyes and the secrets he carried. About the man I'd seen watching the café yesterday.

"Let me know if those instincts turn into anything concrete," I said.

"You'll be the first call." She headed for her usual table, and I tried to shake off the unease that had settled in my chest.

A few tourists trickled in around nine, drawn by the promise of warmth and caffeine, exclaiming over the cats in the adoption room. One of them, a young woman with bright red hair and a warm smile, fell immediately in love with Penny and Copper.

"They're siblings?" she asked, watching them tumble over each other in a play fight. "I couldn't possibly separate them."

"They come as a pair," I confirmed. "We don't split bonded cats."

"Perfect. I've been looking for two cats to keep each other company while I'm at work." She pulled out her phone. "Can I fill out an application?"

It was moments like these that made the café worth every early morning and late night. Watching someone find their perfect match. Knowing that two more cats would have a loving home.

"Told you," Poppy said softly from her heated bed. "Someone was coming for them. I felt it."

Lily handled the application process while I managed the counter. The morning rush was lighter than usual, probably due to the weather. Snow was falling steadily now, fat flakes that stuck to the windows and muffled the sounds of the street outside.

At nine-thirty, Atticus Monroe walked through the door.

I hadn't expected to see him. He was supposed to be on the trails with Grant until at least noon. But here he was, stomping snow from his boots, his expression troubled.

"Atticus? Everything okay?"

"Yeah, but we had to cut the hike short due to the snow coming in."

"Ah, so what can I get you?"

"Coffee. Black. Strong." He dropped onto a stool at the counter, pulling off his gloves. "That writer friend of yours is strange, Alexis."

My stomach tightened. "What happened?"

"We did the hike. Showed him the falls, the overlook, the main trails." Atticus wrapped his hands around the coffee I'd placed in front of him. "But he wasn't interested in any of that. Kept asking about the caves. The hidden spots. Places where someone might..." He paused, searching for the right word. "Hide something."

"Hide something?"

"That's what he said. For his book, supposedly. He wanted to write about secret places, spots only locals know about." Atticus shook his head. "I've met a lot of travel writers over the years. They ask about views, about photo opportunities, about the best times to visit. They don't ask about hiding spots."

"Did you show him?"

"Some of them. The caves near the north trail, the rock formations by the creek. He took notes, asked questions about access, about how often people go there." Atticus took a long drink of his coffee. "And then, when we got back to the main overlook, he said he wanted to stay. Take some more photos, do some exploring on his own."

"You left him up there? In this weather?"

"He insisted. Said he'd be fine, he had supplies, he knew the way back." Atticus met my eyes. "I didn't like it, Alexis. Something about the whole thing felt wrong. But I couldn't exactly force him to leave."

"No," I agreed. "You couldn't."

"I told him to be careful. Told him the storm was going to get worse by afternoon. He said he understood." Atticus set down his empty cup. "But the way he looked when I left him there... he wasn't planning to take photos. He was planning something else."

"What do you think he's really doing up there?"

"I don't know. But if I had to guess?" Atticus pulled his gloves back on, preparing to leave. "I'd say he's looking for something. Or hiding something. Maybe both."

After he left, Lily joined me at the counter.

"I heard most of that," she said quietly. "What do you think?"

"I think Grant Granger has been lying to everyone since he got here. And I think whatever he's mixed up in is about to come to a head."

"Should we tell Iris?"

I considered it. But tell her what? That a travel writer asked strange questions on a hike? That wasn't a crime. It wasn't even suspicious, really. Just... odd.

"Not yet," I decided. "Let's see what happens when he comes back."

The door chimed, and I looked up, half-expecting Grant himself. But it was Lionel, brushing snow from his shoulders, his green eyes bright despite the gray morning.

"Just grabbing my usual to go," he said, approaching the counter. "Busy day at the shop. New shipment came in, and I've got inventory to sort."

I reached for the dandelion root blend. "You're up early."

"Couldn't sleep." He smiled, but there was something tentative in it. "I heard you have a big evening planned."

Small towns. Of course he'd heard.

"Dinner with Colton," I confirmed, keeping my voice neutral. "At that Italian place in Silverpine."

"I've heard good things about it." He accepted his tea, and for just a moment, his fingers brushed against mine. "I hope you have a nice time, Alexis. You deserve a nice evening."

There was no bitterness in his voice. No jealousy. Just genuine warmth, the same warmth he always showed. He meant it. He actually meant it.

"Thank you, Lionel."

"Sure." He tucked the cup into his hand, already turning toward the door. "See you around."

I watched him go, something complicated stirring in my chest. But before I could examine it too closely, the door chimed again.

Grant Granger walked in.

I noticed immediately that something was different. His usual nervous energy had intensified into something closer to panic. His jacket was damp with melted snow, his hair disheveled, and his hands were shaking as he approached the counter.

"Morning, Grant. I didn't expect to see you back so soon."

"Change of plans." He fumbled with his wallet, dropping it twice before managing to extract some bills. "Coffee. Double shot. Please."

"Everything okay? Atticus was just here. He said you wanted to stay on the trails longer."

Grant's head snapped up. "Atticus was here? What did he say?"

"Just that you seemed interested in the caves. The hidden spots."

Something flickered across Grant's face. Fear, I thought. Or maybe resignation.

"Research," he said. "For the book."

"Right. The book."

I made his coffee while he hovered at the counter, not moving toward his usual table. His laptop bag was slung over his shoulder, and he kept adjusting the strap like it was bothering him.

"Actually," he said as I handed him the cup, "I was wondering if I could ask you a favor."

"Of course. What do you need?"

He hesitated, shifting his weight from foot to foot. Then he reached into his bag and pulled out his laptop.

"I need to go back out there. To the falls." He set the laptop on the counter between us. "Would you mind keeping an eye on this for me? I don't want to risk it getting wet or damaged. The trails can be slippery, and if I fell..."

"You're going back? In this weather?"

"I have to." His voice was tight. "I forgot to check something. Verify some details. It won't take long."

"Grant..." I took the laptop, noting how reluctant he seemed to let it go. His fingers lingered on the case for just a moment too long before he released it. "What's really going on?"

For a moment, I thought he might tell me. Something in his expression cracked, just slightly, and I saw the exhausted, frightened man beneath the nervous facade.

But then the wall went back up.

"I'll be back this afternoon. Before you close, definitely." He picked up his coffee with both hands, as if steadying himself. "You've been really helpful, Alexis. I appreciate it. This town, everyone here... you've all been so welcoming."

There was something in his voice that made the words sound less like gratitude and more like goodbye.

"Be careful out there," I called after him as he headed for the door. "The falls can be dangerous this time of year. Ice on the trails, cold water..."

"I'll be careful. I promise." He paused at the door, looking back at me with an expression I couldn't quite read. "Thanks again. For everything."

The bell chimed as he left, and I watched him walk down Main Street, hunched against the falling snow, until he disappeared around the corner.

The door chimed almost immediately after. A man stepped in, medium build, brown hair going gray, the kind of face your eyes would slide right past without catching. He paused just inside the entrance, his gaze moving quickly across the room. Then, without ordering anything, he turned and left.

*Odd*, I thought, but the door was already closing behind him and there were other customers to tend to.

"That was strange," Lily said, appearing at my elbow. "Grant, I mean. He seemed even more wound up than before."

"He went up to the falls with Atticus this morning. Now he's going back alone." I looked down at the laptop in my hands. It was heavier than I expected, a solid weight that felt somehow significant. "Something happened up there. Something that scared him even more than he already was."

"What are you going to do?"

"Nothing I can do. He's an adult. He can hike wherever he wants." I carried the laptop to the back room and tucked it on a shelf behind some supplies. Out of sight, but not out of mind. "But I'm going to keep this safe for him. Whatever's on here, he didn't want it with him up there."

The cats had noticed the tension.

"The secret-smelling human was very afraid today," Poppy said when I returned to the main room. "More afraid than before. More afraid than I've ever smelled anyone."

"Afraid of what?"

"Something coming. Something he's been expecting for a long time." She licked her paw thoughtfully. "I think it finally caught up with him."

The morning crowd thinned as the snow continued to fall. By noon, the street outside was blanketed in white, and only the most determined customers braved the weather. Jasper Sharpe came in around one o'clock, stomping snow from his boots and grumbling about the cold.

"Worst February we've had in years," he said, accepting his usual dark roast. "My joints are predicting at least another six inches before nightfall."

"Your joints are usually right."

"More accurate than any weatherman." He took a sip of his coffee and sighed contentedly. "At least business is good. People stocking up on supplies before they get snowed in."

"Speaking of customers," I said, trying to sound casual, "have you seen Grant Granger lately? The travel writer?"

Jasper's expression flickered. "Saw him twice today, actually. Early this morning, heading up toward the trailhead. Then again about an hour ago, buying more supplies. Energy bars, a flashlight, rope."

"Rope?"

"That's what caught my attention too. Strange thing to need for a hike." Jasper shrugged. "Had a bit of trouble with him last week, to be honest."

"What kind of trouble?"

"His check bounced. First time that's happened with him." Jasper finished his coffee and set the cup on the counter. "He came back the next day, apologized up and down, paid in cash plus a little extra for my trouble. Said it was a banking error, something with a transfer that didn't go through in time."

"Did you believe him?"

"Seemed sincere enough. And he made it right, which is what matters." He paused at the door. "Why do you ask?"

"No reason. Just curious."

But the information filed itself away in my mind, another piece of a puzzle I didn't yet understand. Bounced checks. Secret caves. Rope.

What was Grant Granger really doing in Larkspur Valley?

The afternoon crept by slowly. The snow continued to fall. Customers came and went in small bursts, shaking off flakes and exclaiming over the warmth of the café. I made drinks, served pastries, and tried not to watch the clock.

Grant had said he'd be back before close. It was now past three, and there was no sign of him.

At four o'clock, I noticed a man sitting alone at one of the corner tables.

I recognized him immediately. The same forgettable face I'd seen yesterday, standing outside on the sidewalk, watching the café between texts on his phone. Medium height, medium build, thinning brown hair going gray. The kind of person you'd forget five minutes after meeting them.

But I hadn't forgotten him. And now here he was, inside, nursing a coffee he'd been working on for the past hour.

"That man in the corner," I murmured to Lily. "He was outside yesterday. Watching."

She glanced over casually, then back at me. "I remember. You mentioned him." She paused. "His aura's the same. Lots of anxiety. Some anger. That same professional edge, like being on alert is just part of who he is."

"Like Grant?"

"Different flavor. Grant's fear was personal, desperate. This man's is more... calculated. Patient." She lowered her voice further. "He's waiting for something. Or someone."

"Grant?"

"Maybe. Or maybe us."

That thought sent a chill down my spine that had nothing to do with the weather.

The man stayed for another hour, watching the room, watching the door, watching me. Every few minutes his eyes would sweep the café before returning to some middle distance. He didn't read. Didn't check his phone. Just sat and observed.

At five, he dropped a few bills on the table and slipped out without a word. I watched him walk down Main Street, head ducked against the snow, until he disappeared into the gray afternoon.

Grant still hadn't returned.

"You keep looking at the door," Lily observed during a quiet moment.

"He said he'd be back before close."

"Maybe he got caught in the weather. Decided to wait it out somewhere."

"Maybe." But I kept thinking about the fear in his eyes, the way he'd looked back at me from the doorway. The goodbye that had sounded like more than just a casual farewell.

"Should we call someone?" Lily asked. "Report him missing?"

"It's only been a few hours. He's an adult. He can hike wherever he wants." The words sounded hollow even as I said them. "We'll give it until morning. If he's not back by then, I'll talk to Iris."

Lily nodded, though she didn't look convinced. "Are you still going to dinner with Colton tonight?"

I'd almost forgotten. In the worry over Grant, the whole reason I'd been nervous this morning had slipped my mind.

"I should probably cancel. With the weather..."

"The weather's not that bad. The roads are clear enough. And you already told him yes." Lily gave me a knowing look. "You're not looking for excuses to back out, are you?"

"No." Yes. Maybe. "I just feel strange going on a date when someone might be lost on a mountain somewhere."

"Someone who isn't your responsibility and who you barely know." Lily's voice was gentle but firm. "Alexis, you can't put your life on hold because of a feeling. Grant is probably fine. And even if he's not, there's nothing you can do about it tonight. The trails are too dangerous to search in the dark and snow."

She was right. I knew she was right. But the unease wouldn't settle.

"Go," Lily said. "Have dinner. Try to enjoy yourself. I'll close up and check on the cats. If anything happens, I'll call you."

I changed in my apartment, trading my work clothes for something nicer. Nothing too fancy, just dark jeans and a blue sweater that Lily had once said brought out my eyes. I brushed my hair, applied minimal makeup, and tried to convince myself that I was looking forward to this.

Because I was, wasn't I? Colton was handsome and kind and interested in me. This was what moving forward looked like. This was what normal people did.

Colton arrived at seven on the dot. He looked good in a charcoal coat and dark jeans, his hazel eyes warm as he smiled at me. In his hands, he held a small bouquet of winter flowers, white roses and pale blue hydrangeas.

"These are for you," he said, handing them over. "I know it's a little old-fashioned, but my mother always said you should bring flowers on a first date."

"They're beautiful." I buried my nose in the roses, breathing in their delicate scent. "Thank you, Colton."

"You're welcome." His smile widened. "You look beautiful, by the way. That color suits you."

"Thank you. You look nice too."

The Italian restaurant in Silverpine was only a twenty-minute drive, but the roads were slick with new snow, so Colton drove carefully. He kept up easy conversation during the drive, asking about the café, about how Lily was settling in, about my plans for the spring menu.

"I was thinking about adding some outdoor seating once the weather warms up," I heard myself saying. "The cats can't go outside, obviously, but it might be nice for customers to have the option."

"That sounds wonderful. Summer evenings in Larkspur Valley are something special. There's this golden light that comes through the mountains around seven o'clock..." He shook his head, smiling. "Sorry. I get poetic about sunsets. Occupational hazard of spending so much time outdoors with animals."

"I like it. Tell me more."

And he did. He talked about the light on the mountains, about the wildflowers that bloomed in the meadows, about the way the whole valley seemed to come alive after the long winter. He had a way of describing things that made me see them, made me feel like I was already there, sitting on that imaginary patio with a cup of coffee, watching the sun go down.

He made it sound so simple. So possible. A future stretching out in front of me, filled with outdoor seating and summer sunsets and normal, everyday things.

I tried to focus on that image instead of the laptop hidden in my back room. Instead of Grant Granger's frightened eyes.

The restaurant was warm and intimate, with checkered tablecloths and candles flickering on every table. Colton held my chair for me, helped me with my coat, and when the waiter appeared, ordered for both of us without consulting the menu.

"We'll start with the bruschetta, and a bottle of the Chianti Classico. The 2019 if you have it." He glanced at me with a smile. "Trust me, it's excellent here. And for dinner, the chicken piccata for the lady, and I'll have the veal marsala."

I blinked. I hadn't even opened my menu yet.

"I hope you don't mind," he said, catching my expression. "I've been here a few times, and I know what's good. The chicken piccata is their best dish. You're going to love it."

Part of me wanted to say that I could order for myself, thank you very much. But another part, a part I wasn't entirely comfortable with, found it almost... nice? To have someone else take charge. To not have to make decisions for once. I spent all day making decisions at the café. Maybe it was okay to let someone else handle things for one evening.

"That sounds fine," I said, and his smile widened.

He was attentive throughout dinner, asking questions about my life, my interests, how I'd ended up in Larkspur Valley. I gave him the sanitized version, the story I told everyone: burned out from city life, wanted a change, found this small town and fell in love with it.

"I know what you mean," he said. "I did my residency in Denver. Great city, great opportunities. But after a while, I just felt... lost in it, you know? Too many people, too much noise. When I came up here for a weekend trip, something clicked. Like the mountains were telling me I was finally in the right place."

"That's exactly how I felt."

"Then we have something in common." He raised his glass, and I raised mine to meet it. "To finding the right place. And maybe the right people."

The dinner was excellent. The chicken piccata Colton had promised lived up to its reputation, and the conversation flowed easily between us. He told me stories about his veterinary practice, including a memorable one about a parrot who had learned to perfectly mimic his receptionist's phone greeting.

"Every time someone called, this parrot would answer first," he said, grinning. "Half our patients thought we'd hired a new staff member with a very distinctive voice."

I laughed, and for a moment, I almost forgot about everything else. Almost.

But then my phone buzzed with a text from Lily: "Still no sign of Grant. Getting worried."

I must have made a face, because Colton's expression shifted to concern.

"Everything okay?"

"Just a customer who didn't come back when he said he would. He went hiking this morning and hasn't returned."

"In this weather?" Colton frowned. "That's not good. Have you reported it?"

"Not yet. It hasn't been that long."

"If someone's been on the trails since this morning, in this cold..." He trailed off, but I understood what he wasn't saying. Exposure was a real danger. The temperature had been dropping all day, and the snow had added wind chill to the equation.

"He's probably fine," I said, though I didn't believe it. "Probably found a cabin or something to wait out the storm."

Colton reached across the table and took my hand. His palm was warm, his grip firm. "You're worried about him."

"I barely know him."

"That doesn't mean you can't be worried." He squeezed my hand. "That's one of the things I like about you, Alexis. You care about people. Even strangers."

"Is that a good thing?"

"It's a wonderful thing. The world needs more people who care." He released my hand and signaled for the waiter. "We're going to skip dessert. Can we get the check?"

"Colton, you don't have to—"

"You're worried. So we're going to do something about it." He said it matter-of-factly, like the decision had already been made. "I'll take you home. You can call the sheriff, file a report, make sure someone knows to look for him."

I wasn't sure if I was grateful or irritated. Maybe both. He was being helpful, taking charge of a situation I'd been dithering about all evening. That was a good thing. Wasn't it?

"Thank you," I said. "That means a lot."

"Of course." He smiled, warm and confident. "That's what I'm here for."

We skipped dessert and headed back to Larkspur Valley. The roads were worse now, thick with fresh snow, and the drive took longer than it should have. Colton focused on the road, both hands on the wheel, but he kept glancing over to make sure I was okay.

By the time we pulled onto Main Street, it was nearly nine o'clock.

The café was dark, closed up for the night. I could see the glow of my apartment windows above, and Lily had left the porch light on.

"Do you want me to come up with you?" Colton asked. "I could wait while you check in with your friend, make sure everything's okay."

"No, I'll be fine. You should get home before the roads get worse." I hesitated. "I don't think I'll go to the station tonight anyway. It's late, and Iris is probably not even there. I'll just call her."

"You're sure? I could drive you over if you change your mind."

"I'm sure." I managed a smile. "Thank you for dinner. And for... handling things. When I got worried."

"Anytime." He leaned in, and for a moment I thought he might try to kiss me. But he just pressed his lips to my cheek, soft and brief. "Goodnight, Alexis. Call me if you need anything. I mean it."

I watched him drive away, then climbed the stairs to my apartment. The evening played back in my mind as I ascended. Colton ordering for me. Colton deciding we should leave. Colton taking charge when I'd gotten worried. He'd been so... certain. So decisive.

Was that a good thing? I honestly wasn't sure. Part of me had found it comforting, like being carried along by a current instead of having to swim. But another part, a smaller part I couldn't quite name, wondered what it would be like if he'd asked instead of told.

I pushed the thought aside. He'd been trying to help. That was what mattered.

Lily was waiting on the couch, a mug of tea in her hands and five cats arranged around her in various poses of concern.

"He didn't come back," she said unnecessarily.

"I know." I sank into the chair across from her. "I'm going to call Iris."

"Now? It's late."

"She told me once that she doesn't sleep much. And if Grant is really missing..." I pulled out my phone and found Iris's number. "Better to start looking sooner than later."

Iris answered on the second ring, sounding alert despite the hour. I explained the situation as concisely as I could: Grant Granger, travel writer, hiked to Aspen Falls with Atticus Monroe early this morning. Came back to town around ten, left again saying he needed to verify something. Said he'd be back before closing. Never returned.

"Atticus was with him this morning?" Iris asked.

"For part of it. Grant insisted on staying behind alone. Then he came back to town and went out again."

"That's concerning." I could hear her writing something down. "I'll have someone check the trailheads first thing in the morning. See if his car is still there. If it is, we'll organize a search party." A pause. "You did the right thing calling me, Alexis. Get some sleep if you can. I'll be in touch."

I hung up and met Lily's eyes across the room.

"She's taking it seriously," I said.

"Good."

But sleep didn't come easily that night. I lay awake listening to the wind howl outside my windows, imagining Grant Granger somewhere out there in the cold. Alone. Afraid.

Clutching secrets he might never get the chance to tell.

And in my back room, his laptop waited. Silent. Locked. Full of answers I couldn't yet access. I hadn't mentioned it to Iris. I wasn't sure why. Maybe because Grant had trusted me with it, had looked at me with those frightened eyes and asked me to keep it safe. Maybe because some instinct told me that whatever was on that laptop was the key to everything.

Or maybe I just wasn't ready to let go of the only piece of Grant Granger I had left.

Morning couldn't come fast enough.

# Chapter Three

I woke before dawn, pulled from restless dreams by a sense of wrongness I couldn't name. The cats were still sleeping, scattered across the bed and various perches around the room. Gus had claimed the pillow next to mine, his black and white bulk radiating warmth. Poppy was curled at my feet. Rocky had somehow wedged himself into the narrow space between my nightstand and the wall. Millie was hidden under the bed, as usual, and Sage had burrowed beneath the blankets until only her tiny gray ears were visible.

I lay there for a moment, listening to the silence outside. The storm had passed sometime in the night, leaving behind a heavy stillness that felt almost oppressive. No howling gusts, no rattling windows. Just quiet.

And somewhere out there, Grant Granger.

I checked my phone. No messages from Iris. No missed calls. But there was a text from Colton, sent at eleven-thirty last night: "Hope you're okay. Let me know if you need anything. Thinking of you."

Simple. Thoughtful. The kind of message a good man sends after a difficult evening.

I typed back a quick reply: "Didn't sleep well but I'm okay. Thank you for checking in."

The response came almost immediately, despite the early hour: "I'm here if you need me. Coffee later?"

I stared at the message for a moment, not sure how to respond. Part of me wanted to say yes, wanted the comfort of his steady presence. But another part felt like accepting would be admitting I couldn't handle things on my own.

"Maybe," I finally wrote. "I'll let you know how the day goes."

"Sounds good. Take care of yourself, Alexis."

I set the phone aside and stared at the ceiling. It was barely five-thirty, too early for any real news. But I couldn't shake the feeling that something had already happened. Something I wouldn't be able to undo.

Sleep was impossible after that. I showered, dressed, and went downstairs to start my morning routine an hour earlier than usual. The café was cold and dark, and I turned on all the lights just to push back the shadows.

"You're up early," Poppy observed, padding down the stairs behind me. "Bad dreams?"

"Something like that."

"The secret human didn't come back."

"No. He didn't."

She settled onto her heated bed, her green eyes watching me with that uncanny perception cats sometimes have. "Something bad happened to him. I can feel it."

"You can feel it?"

"The air tastes wrong this morning. Like fear and endings." She curled her tail around her paws. "I don't like it."

Neither did I.

The other cats trickled downstairs over the next hour, drawn by the smell of coffee and the promise of breakfast. I fed them, checked on the adoption room cats, and tried to keep myself busy with tasks that didn't require much thought. Restocking napkins. Wiping down tables. Arranging the pastry display even though Flo's delivery wouldn't arrive for another hour.

And in the back room, Grant's laptop sat on its shelf. Waiting. I'd checked on it twice already, as if it might have disappeared in the night. As if someone might have come for it while I slept.

Maybe I should have told Iris about it. Maybe I still should. But something held me back. Grant had trusted me with it. Had looked at me with those frightened eyes and asked me to keep it safe.

Whatever secrets were locked behind that password, they were mine to protect now.

Lily came in at seven, her expression worried.

"Any news?"

"Nothing yet." I handed her an apron. "Iris said she'd have someone check the trailheads this morning."

"That's good. That's something." But she didn't sound convinced, and I couldn't blame her.

The morning crawled by. Customers came and went, oblivious to the tension that had settled over me like a second skin. Mabel arrived at her usual time, ordered her usual tea, and opened her crossword puzzle without comment. A few tourists stopped in, drawn by our reputation and the promise of cats. One of them spent twenty minutes in the adoption room, cooing over Whiskers.

I kept watching the door. Waiting for Grant to walk through it, laptop bag over his shoulder, apologizing for worrying everyone. Waiting for this whole thing to be a misunderstanding, a false alarm, a story we'd laugh about later.

But Grant didn't come.

At nine-fifteen, Sheriff Iris Scott walked through the door.

I knew immediately that something was wrong. It wasn't just her expression, though that was grim enough. It was the way she moved, deliberate and heavy, like someone carrying news they didn't want to deliver. She didn't go to the counter to order her usual coffee. Instead, she walked directly to where I stood near the espresso machine, her eyes meeting mine with a look that made my stomach drop.

"Alexis. Is there somewhere we can talk privately?"

"The back room." My voice came out steadier than I felt. "Lily, can you watch the counter?"

Lily nodded, her face pale. She'd seen Iris's expression too.

I led the sheriff to the small storage room behind the kitchen. It wasn't much, just shelves of supplies and a tiny desk where I did paperwork, but it was private. I closed the door behind us and waited, acutely aware of Grant's laptop sitting on the shelf not three feet from where Iris stood.

Iris didn't waste time with pleasantries.

"We found Grant Granger this morning. At Aspen Falls." She paused, and in that pause I heard everything she wasn't saying. "He's dead, Alexis. I'm sorry."

The words landed like stones, heavy and final. I'd known, somehow. From the moment I'd woken up with that sense of wrongness, I'd known. But hearing it spoken aloud made it real in a way that suspicion never could.

"How?" The question came out as a whisper.

"We're still investigating. But it wasn't an accident." Iris's jaw tightened. "There were signs of a struggle on the trail above the falls. And the medical examiner's preliminary assessment suggests he was dead before he hit the water."

"Someone killed him."

"That's what it looks like." She pulled out a small notebook, the same one she always carried. "You called me last night about him being missing. I need to know everything you can tell me about Grant Granger. How long had he been coming here? Did he seem different lately? Mention anyone he was worried about?"

"He'd been a regular for about two and a half weeks. Always came in with his laptop, always sat by the window." I thought carefully about what to share, my eyes carefully not drifting to the shelf behind Iris. "He seemed nervous from the start, but it got worse over the past few days. Like he was waiting for something bad to happen."

"Did he say anything specific? Mention anyone by name?"

"No. Just that he was working on a book about mountain towns. Research, he said." The words sounded hollow now, the lie they'd probably always been. "But I don't think he was really writing a book. I think he was hiding from something. Or someone."

Iris made a note. "Anything else? Anyone who came looking for him? Anyone suspicious?"

I thought about the man in the corner yesterday, the one with the forgettable face and the professional anxiety. The one who'd been watching the café from outside on Tuesday before coming inside on Wednesday.

"There was someone. A man I didn't recognize." I described him as best I could, which wasn't well. He'd been designed to be unremarkable, the kind of person your eyes slid right past. "Medium height, medium build, thinning brown hair going gray. I first noticed him Tuesday afternoon, standing outside the café, watching through the window. Then yesterday he came inside. Sat in the corner for over an hour, nursing a single coffee, not reading, not looking at his phone. Just watching."

Iris looked up sharply. "Two days in a row?"

"Yes. Lily noticed him too. She said his... demeanor was off. Anxious, but in a practiced way. Like he was used to being on edge."

"Like someone used to surveillance," Iris said quietly, more to herself than to me. She made several notes. "Anyone else? Anyone local acting strangely around Grant?"

I hesitated. "Atticus mentioned something yesterday. He took Grant hiking in the morning, before Grant came back to town. He said

Grant was asking strange questions. About caves, hiding spots, places most people don't know about."

"I'll talk to Atticus." Iris paused. "What about Vernon Holt? Did Grant ever mention him?"

The name surprised me. "Vernon? The man who lives up near the falls? No, Grant never mentioned him. Why?"

"Vernon filed a complaint two days ago. Said a tourist was trespassing on his property, poking around where he didn't belong. Description matches Grant Granger." Iris's expression was unreadable. "Vernon's got a temper. Everyone knows that. And he's very protective of his land."

"You think Vernon might have..."

"I'm not thinking anything yet. Just gathering information." She closed her notebook. "I'll be in touch if I have more questions. And Alexis?" She paused at the door. "This is the third murder in Larkspur Valley in less than a year. People are going to be scared. Probably angry too. If you hear anything, see anything, notice anything out of the ordinary, you call me. Understood?"

"Understood."

She reached for the door handle, then stopped. "One more thing. Did Grant leave anything with you? Any belongings?"

My heart stuttered. The laptop was right there, three feet away, hidden behind a stack of napkin boxes. All Iris had to do was turn around and look.

"No," I heard myself say. "Nothing."

The lie came out smooth, automatic. I wasn't even sure why I said it. But once the word was out, I couldn't take it back.

Iris studied me for a moment, her cop's eyes sharp and assessing. Then she nodded.

"Alright. Take care of yourself, Alexis. And be careful. Until we know what's going on, everyone should be watching their backs."

After she left, I stood in the back room for a long moment, staring at the laptop on its shelf. I'd just lied to the sheriff. Withheld evidence in a murder investigation. If Iris found out, she'd never trust me again.

But Grant had trusted me. Had looked at me with those frightened eyes and asked me to keep his laptop safe. Whatever was on it, whatever secrets it contained, he hadn't wanted them falling into the wrong hands.

The question was: whose hands were the wrong ones?

I picked up the laptop, turning it over. It looked so ordinary. A standard business laptop with a few stickers on the case. But somewhere inside this machine were answers. The reason Grant had been afraid. The reason someone had killed him.

I just had to figure out how to access them.

When I returned to the main room, Lily was waiting with questions in her eyes. I shook my head slightly, a signal that we'd talk later, when we didn't have customers within earshot.

But news travels fast in small towns.

By ten o'clock, word had spread. Customers came in not just for coffee but for information, gathering in small clusters to exchange what little they knew. The travel writer was dead. Found at the falls. Murdered, some said, though others insisted it must have been an accident. The trails were dangerous this time of year. People fell all the time.

But I saw the fear beneath the speculation. Larkspur Valley was supposed to be safe. A quiet mountain town where nothing bad happened. Hazel's murder last fall had shaken that illusion, and now Grant's death had shattered it completely.

Through the window, I saw Lionel crossing the street from his comic shop. He paused outside the café, looking in, and our eyes met through the glass. He didn't come inside. Just raised his hand in a small wave, his expression full of quiet concern. A question: Are you okay?

I nodded, and he nodded back. Then he continued on his way, leaving me with an unexpected warmth in my chest.

No pressure. No demands. Just a silent check-in, a reminder that someone was thinking of me.

Cordelia burst through the door around ten-thirty, her colorful scarves fluttering behind her like agitated birds.

"Is it true?" she demanded, not bothering with a greeting. "The travel writer? Dead at the falls?"

"It's true," I said quietly.

"But how? Why?" She pressed a hand to her chest, genuinely distressed. "He was just in here yesterday! I saw him walking down Main Street. He waved at me!"

"I don't know, Cordelia. The sheriff is investigating."

"Investigating! As if that helped poor Hazel!" She sank into the nearest chair, fanning herself with her hand. "What's happening to this town? First Hazel, then that business with Warren, and now this. It's like we're cursed."

"We're not cursed," I said, though I understood her fear. "Bad things happen everywhere. Even in places like Larkspur Valley."

"They didn't used to." Her voice was small, suddenly old. "I've lived here my whole life. Seventy-two years. And until last fall, I'd never known anyone who was murdered."

"I heard Vernon Holt had a run-in with that writer," Jasper said, appearing at the counter for his mid-morning coffee. "Filed a complaint about trespassing."

Cordelia's eyes went wide. "Vernon? You don't think..."

"I don't think anything," Jasper said quickly. "Just saying what I heard. Vernon's always been territorial about that property of his. Doesn't mean he's a killer."

"But he has that temper," Cordelia said. "Remember when he got into it with old Mr. Leland over the property line? Threatened to shoot his dog if it came on his land again."

"That was twenty years ago, Cordelia."

"A temper like that doesn't just go away."

I made Cordelia a cup of chamomile tea, extra strong, and let her sit in the warmth of the café until she felt steady enough to leave. But her words stayed with me. Vernon Holt. Territorial. A temper that didn't just go away.

Had Grant stumbled onto something on Vernon's property? Something worth killing to protect?

The lunch rush was subdued. People ordered their drinks and food, but the usual cheerful chatter was replaced by hushed conversations and worried glances. Everyone had theories. Everyone had questions. And no one had answers.

At two o'clock, Atticus Monroe walked through the door.

I'd been expecting him, in a way. He was the one who patrolled those trails, who knew the falls better than anyone. If anyone had found Grant's body, it would have been Atticus.

But I wasn't expecting the look on his face.

He was pale beneath his tan, his movements stiff and careful like someone nursing an injury that didn't show. He came to the counter and ordered his usual black coffee, but when I handed it to him, his hands were trembling.

"Atticus? Are you okay?"

"I found him." His voice was flat, distant. "This morning. I was doing my usual patrol, and I found him."

"I'm so sorry. That must have been awful."

"It was." He stared into his coffee, not drinking. "But that's not... that's not the worst part."

I waited, sensing there was more.

"Something strange happened." He looked up at me, and there was something in his eyes I hadn't seen before. Fear, yes, but also confusion. Uncertainty. Like a man whose understanding of the world had just shifted beneath his feet. "Before I found him. When I was still on the trail."

"What kind of strange?"

He was quiet for a long moment, wrestling with something. Around us, the café hummed with the low murmur of conversation, but it felt like we were in our own bubble, separated from everything else.

"There was a hawk," he finally said. "Circling above the falls. I see hawks out there all the time. It's not unusual. But this one was different. Agitated. Upset. And when I looked at it..." He trailed off, shaking his head.

"What happened when you looked at it?"

"I saw something. Felt something." He set down his coffee cup, his hands still unsteady. "Violence. Fear. A face I didn't recognize. It was like... like the hawk was showing me what it had seen. What had happened there."

My breath caught. I knew exactly what he was describing. I'd grown up in a coven, surrounded by magic, understanding my gift from childhood. But I'd heard stories about people like Atticus, people who had abilities they didn't understand, who spent years rationalizing away what they experienced. That moment when the door finally cracked open, when they couldn't explain it away anymore, was supposed to be transformative. And terrifying.

"Atticus," I said carefully, "what do you think happened?"

"I don't know." He laughed, but there was no humor in it. "I've spent my whole life in these woods. I've always been good with animals. Better than good. They trust me, listen to me. Sometimes I swear they understand what I'm saying." He met my eyes. "But this was different. This wasn't understanding. This was... communication. Real communication. Like the hawk was trying to tell me something."

"And what did it tell you?"

"Where to look." His voice dropped to barely a whisper. "I followed the feeling. Followed the hawk. And it led me straight to Grant's body."

We stared at each other across the counter. I wanted to tell him that I understood, that I knew exactly what he was experiencing, that he wasn't crazy or imagining things. But this wasn't the time or place. Not with customers nearby, not with a murder investigation just beginning.

"That sounds terrifying," I said instead. "Finding a body like that."

"It was." He picked up his coffee again, took a long sip. "I keep seeing his face. Grant's face. And I keep feeling what the hawk felt. This... rage and fear, all mixed together. Like echoes that won't fade."

"Have you told anyone else? About the hawk, I mean?"

"No. Who would I tell? Iris would think I'd lost my mind. The other rangers would laugh me out of the station." He shook his head. "It's probably just stress. Shock from finding the body. My brain playing tricks on me."

"Maybe," I said. "Or maybe it's something else."

He looked at me sharply. "What do you mean?"

"I mean..." I hesitated, choosing my words carefully. "I mean that sometimes things happen that we can't explain. Things that don't fit into neat categories. And just because we can't explain them doesn't mean they're not real."

Something flickered in his eyes. Recognition, maybe. Or hope.

"You sound like you know what you're talking about."

"Maybe I do." I glanced around the café, confirming that no one was paying attention to us. "Listen, if you want to talk more about this, you should go see Maeve at The Turning Page."

"Maeve?" He looked surprised. "The bookshop owner? I know her, but what would she..."

"She understands things that are hard to explain. More than most people." I held his gaze. "Trust me. If anyone in this town can help you make sense of what you're experiencing, it's her."

"I might take you up on that," he said. "Once all this settles down. Once the investigation..." He trailed off, looking suddenly exhausted. "I should go. I have to give my statement again. Go over everything a dozen more times for the detectives."

"Before you go," I said, keeping my voice casual. "Iris mentioned Vernon Holt filed a complaint about Grant trespassing. Did you see anything when you took Grant hiking yesterday? Any sign of Vernon?"

Atticus's expression darkened. "I saw Vernon, yeah. Up on the ridge above the north trail. He was watching us through binoculars." He paused. "And when Grant wandered off toward the property line, Vernon came down and had words with him. Told him to stay off his land if he knew what was good for him."

"What did Grant do?"

"Apologized. Said he didn't realize where the boundaries were. But Vernon wasn't having it. Got right up in Grant's face, jabbing his finger at him." Atticus shook his head. "I've known Vernon for years. He's always been prickly, but I've never seen him that angry. It was like Grant had personally offended him somehow."

"Did you tell Iris about this?"

"First thing this morning. She said she'd look into it."

After Atticus left, I stood behind the counter, my mind churning. Vernon Holt confronting Grant on the trail. The mysterious watching man who'd appeared twice in two days. Grant's laptop, hidden in my back room, full of secrets I couldn't access.

And somewhere in all of it, the truth about why Grant Granger had come to Larkspur Valley. And why someone had killed him.

The rest of the afternoon passed in a blur of coffee and condolences. People kept coming in, wanting to talk about Grant, about the murder, about what it meant for Larkspur Valley. I made drinks and listened and offered what comfort I could, all while my mind churned with questions I couldn't answer.

At six o'clock, I flipped the sign to Closed and locked the front door. Lily and I cleaned up in silence, both of us processing the day in our own ways. The cats, sensing the mood, were quieter than usual, clustering near me instead of spreading out through the café.

"The town feels different," Poppy said as I wiped down the counter. "Heavier. Sadder."

"Someone died," I said. "Someone was killed."

"The secret human."

"Yes. Grant."

Poppy was quiet for a moment. "He was scared for a reason. Whatever he was hiding, someone wanted it badly enough to kill him."

"I know."

"Will you find out who?"

I thought about Iris, working the case through official channels. About the laptop, still hidden in my back room, full of secrets I had no idea how to unlock. About Atticus, stumbling onto his gift in the worst possible circumstances. About Vernon Holt with his temper and his territorial rage. About the watching man with his forgettable face and his professional patience.

"I don't know," I admitted. "But I have a feeling I won't be able to stay out of it."

Gus jumped onto the counter beside me, something he knew he wasn't supposed to do. But tonight I didn't have the energy to scold him.

"Good," he said. "The bad humans need to be found. And you're better at finding them than anyone else."

I wasn't sure that was true. But I also wasn't sure it mattered. Grant Granger was dead, murdered at Aspen Falls. And somewhere in Larkspur Valley, his killer was walking free.

That wasn't something I could ignore.

Even if it meant putting myself in danger again.

Even if it meant facing whatever darkness had followed Grant to this quiet mountain town.

Some things were more important than staying safe.

Justice, for one.

The truth, for another.

And making sure that whoever had killed Grant Granger didn't get the chance to hurt anyone else.

# Chapter Four

Friday morning brought clear skies and a fresh blanket of snow that made Larkspur Valley look like something from a postcard. The kind of pristine, peaceful beauty that attracted tourists and convinced people that nothing bad could ever happen here.

But something bad had happened. And the whole town knew it.

I opened the café at the usual time, moving through my routine with a heaviness that hadn't lifted since Iris delivered the news. The cats followed me downstairs, having spent the night in their usual positions around my bed. Gus had claimed the pillow next to mine, Poppy at my feet, Rocky wedged against my side.

"You tossed and turned all night," Poppy said as she settled onto her heated bed. "I counted at least twelve position changes."

"Fourteen," Gus corrected, jumping onto his favorite perch. "And she kept sighing. Very disruptive to my sleep."

"I'm sorry," I said. "I couldn't stop thinking."

"About the secret human," Poppy said. It wasn't a question.

"About everything."

Rocky bounded past, still somehow energetic despite the restless night. "I tried to help! I purred extra loud. Did it help?"

"It did, Rocky. Thank you."

Sage emerged from behind the cat tree near the window. "The bad feelings were very loud last night. In the air. I didn't like them."

I scooped her up and held her close for a moment. She was getting bigger, but she still fit in my hands. "I know, sweetheart. I didn't like them either."

"There's something else too," Poppy said quietly. "Something in the air that doesn't belong. I noticed it yesterday, and it's still here."

"What do you mean?"

"I don't know exactly. It's not the murder feeling. It's something... older. Watching." She flicked her tail uneasily. "I don't like it."

I wanted to dismiss it as Poppy being overly sensitive to the town's collective anxiety. But something about her words resonated with a feeling I'd been trying to ignore. A prickle at the back of my neck that had nothing to do with Grant Granger or his secrets.

I pushed it aside. There was enough to worry about without borrowing trouble.

My phone buzzed with a text from Colton: "Heard the news about the murder. Are you okay? I know he was a regular at your café. Call me if you need to talk."

I typed back: "I'm okay. It's been a lot to process. Thanks for checking in."

His response came quickly: "Of course. I'm here for you, Alexis. Whatever you need."

Whatever you need. It was a nice sentiment. The kind of thing a good man says when he's trying to be supportive. I should have felt comforted by it.

Instead, I felt vaguely pressured, though I couldn't have explained why.

Lily arrived at seven, looking as tired as I felt. We exchanged the kind of wordless greeting that had become common between us, a shared acknowledgment that things were not okay and might not be okay for a while.

"I talked to Maeve last night," she said quietly, once we were both behind the counter. "About Atticus."

"Good. He came to see me yesterday, after he gave his statement. He was shaken." I lowered my voice further. "He told me about the hawk. How it showed him things, led him to Grant's body. He doesn't understand what's happening to him."

"Maeve said she's been watching him for years. Waiting for him to figure it out on his own." Lily pulled her hair back into a ponytail, her movements efficient and practiced. "She thinks the hawk experience was the catalyst. When it showed him the violence, the fear. That's when his gift truly woke up."

"And then finding the body right after..."

"Confirmed it wasn't just his imagination." Lily nodded. "He can't explain it away anymore. Not when the hawk led him straight to Grant."

"I told him to go see Maeve. That she understands things that are hard to explain."

"She mentioned that. She's hoping he'll come by soon." Lily paused. "She thinks once the door opens, it's hard to close it again. He's going to need guidance."

"We all did, at first."

The morning rush was busier than yesterday, which surprised me. I'd expected people to stay home, to hunker down in the wake of the murder. Instead, they seemed to crave connection, the comfort of familiar faces and warm drinks and the illusion that everything was normal.

Or maybe they just wanted to gossip.

"I heard he wasn't even a real travel writer," one customer told another, loud enough for half the café to hear. "Mildred at the post office said he was receiving mail under three different names."

"Three names?" Her companion raised her eyebrows. "That's suspicious."

"More than suspicious. That's criminal behavior."

At the next table, two men were having a similar conversation.

"My cousin works at the Pine Lodge. Says Grant paid for everything in cash. Two weeks in advance, no questions asked."

"Cash? Who carries that much cash around?"

"Someone who doesn't want to be traced."

I listened without commenting, filing away each piece of information for later. Some of it was probably exaggeration, the details inflating with each retelling. But some of it might be useful.

"I heard Vernon Holt had some kind of confrontation with him," Cordelia announced when she came in for her morning chamomile. "Up on the trails. Vernon was screaming about trespassers, threatening all sorts of things."

"Who told you that?" I asked.

"Beatrice from the quilting circle. Her husband was hiking that day, saw the whole thing." Cordelia leaned in conspiratorially. "Vernon was practically foaming at the mouth, she said. Had to be restrained from getting physical."

I filed that away too, though I suspected the story had grown in the telling. Still, it matched what Atticus had said about Vernon confronting Grant on the trail.

Around ten o'clock, I noticed a familiar figure walking past the window.

The watching man. The one with the forgettable face and the professional patience.

He didn't come in this time. Just walked past slowly, glancing through the window, his eyes sweeping the interior of the café before continuing down the street. But I saw him. And I was certain he saw me too.

"Lily." I kept my voice low. "That man. The one who was watching yesterday. He just walked past."

She moved to the window casually, pretending to adjust the display of pastries. "I don't see anyone."

"He's gone now. But he was there. Looking in."

"Should we tell Iris?"

"And say what? That a man walked past our window?" I shook my head. "We have nothing concrete. Just feelings."

"Your feelings are usually right."

"I know. But feelings don't hold up in court."

Around eleven o'clock, a woman I didn't recognize walked through the door.

She was in her late thirties, with sharp features and sharper eyes. Her blonde hair was pulled back in a severe ponytail, and she wore the kind of practical clothing that suggested she'd dressed for function rather than fashion. Everything about her screamed tension, from her rigid posture to the way her gaze swept the café like she was cataloging threats.

"Can I help you?" I asked as she approached the counter.

"I'm looking for someone." Her voice was clipped, controlled. "A man named Grant Granger. I was told he frequented this café."

I felt Lily stiffen beside me. We exchanged a quick glance before I turned back to the woman.

"I'm sorry, who are you?"

"Dina Marsh." She didn't offer her hand. "Grant and I were... involved. A while back. I've been trying to track him down for months."

"I'm afraid I have some bad news, Ms. Marsh." I kept my voice gentle, the way I'd learned to deliver difficult information. "Grant Granger passed away. His body was found yesterday at Aspen Falls."

The emotions that crossed her face were complex and difficult to read. Shock, certainly. But also anger, and something that might have been bitter satisfaction.

"Dead?" She laughed, a harsh sound without humor. "That lying bastard actually managed to get himself killed?"

"I'm sorry for your loss."

"Don't be." She leaned against the counter, suddenly looking exhausted rather than aggressive. "Grant Granger stole forty thousand dollars from me. Convinced me he was investing it, building a future for us. Then he disappeared in the middle of the night with every cent."

I didn't know what to say to that. The Grant I'd known, nervous and secretive as he was, hadn't seemed like a con artist. But then again, the best con artists never did.

"When did this happen?" Lily asked.

"Eight months ago. I've been tracking him ever since." Dina's jaw tightened. "I was getting close. Finally had a lead that put him here, in this little town. And now you're telling me he's dead?"

"The sheriff is investigating," I said. "If you have information about Grant, she'd probably want to talk to you."

"Oh, I'll be talking to the sheriff. I have plenty to say about Grant Granger." Her eyes narrowed. "How was he killed? The woman at the lodge just said there was an accident at the falls."

"The sheriff believes it was murder."

Something flickered in Dina's expression. Surprise, maybe. Or calculation. "Murder. So someone else got to him first."

"What do you mean, first?"

"I mean I fantasized about killing him for months after he took my money. Made elaborate plans I never intended to carry out." She shrugged, unapologetic. "But I wanted my money back. Dead men can't write checks."

It was a cold way to put it. But there was a practicality beneath the anger that made me think she was telling the truth. Dina Marsh wanted justice, or at least restitution. Revenge without recovery didn't serve her purposes.

"Did Grant have enemies?" I asked. "Anyone who might have wanted him dead?"

"Besides me?" She laughed bitterly. "I'm sure he had plenty. Men like Grant don't just swindle one woman. There were others before me, and probably others after. He was good at what he did. Charming. Convincing." Her expression hardened. "Made you feel special right up until the moment he disappeared with everything you had."

"Do you know any of their names? The other women he conned?"

"I found two of them online. Support forums for fraud victims." Dina's voice softened slightly. "One woman in Phoenix lost her retirement savings. Another in Seattle lost her house. He used different names with each of us, but the pattern was the same. Romance, promises, then gone."

"Did any of them come looking for him?"

"The woman in Phoenix died last year. Cancer. The one in Seattle has three kids and can barely afford groceries, let alone a cross-country manhunt." Dina paused. "But those are just the ones I found. There could be dozens more. And not all of them were lonely women."

"What do you mean?"

"There were rumors. Online, in some of the forums where victims share information." Dina lowered her voice. "People said Grant had gotten in over his head. That he'd stolen from someone bigger than lonely women with savings accounts. Someone dangerous."

"What kind of dangerous?"

"The kind with lawyers and accountants and people who make problems disappear. Corporate money, maybe. Or worse." She pulled a card from her pocket and set it on the counter. "I'm staying at the Pine Lodge for a few more days. If you remember anything about Grant, anything at all, call me. I want to know what he was doing here. What he was hiding."

"I'll keep that in mind."

"One more thing." She hesitated. "There was a man asking questions at the lodge this morning. Average looking, forgettable face. He wanted to know which room Grant had been staying in."

My heart stuttered. "What did you tell him?"

"Nothing. I don't talk to strangers who ask too many questions." She gave me a long look, like she was trying to decide whether to trust me. "But he's still around. I saw him walking down Main Street an hour ago. If Grant really did steal from dangerous people, that man might be one of them."

After she was gone, Lily let out a breath. "Well. That was something."

"Grant was a con artist." I picked up Dina's card, turning it over in my hands. "That explains a lot. The fear. The secrecy. The looking over his shoulder."

"He wasn't just hiding. He was running from people he'd wronged."

"People like Dina. But maybe others too." I thought about what she'd said. Corporate money. People who make problems disappear. "The watching man was asking about Grant at the lodge. He's definitely connected to this somehow."

The cats had been listening from their various perches. Poppy jumped down and wound around my ankles.

"The angry woman wasn't lying," she said. "I could tell. She wanted her money back, not blood."

"You could tell?"

"Her anger was cold, not hot. Calculating. She wanted something from him, not just to hurt him." Poppy flicked her tail. "The ones who kill for revenge smell different. More desperate."

"Which means if she didn't kill Grant, someone else did." I looked at Lily. "Someone who wanted more than money. Or someone who wanted the money Grant stole from them."

"The dangerous people Dina mentioned," Lily said quietly. "The ones with resources."

"And possibly a forgettable man who asks too many questions."

The afternoon was quieter, the gossip dying down as people returned to their normal routines. But I couldn't stop thinking about what Dina had said. About dangerous people who send others to do their dirty work. About Grant being in over his head.

The laptop was still hidden in my back room. Still full of secrets I hadn't uncovered. And suddenly that felt less like evidence I was protecting and more like a target I was holding.

"We should move it," I said to Lily during a quiet moment. "The laptop. It's not safe here."

"Where would we take it?"

"Maeve's. The bookshop has a thousand hiding places, and she has wards that would alert her if anyone with bad intentions tried to enter."

Lily nodded slowly. "That makes sense. If Dina tracked Grant here, others might too. And they might know he spent time at this café."

"We'll do it tonight. After dark. Less chance of being seen."

The rest of the day passed in a haze of coffee and worry. I kept glancing at the back room, kept thinking about the laptop and what secrets it held. Grant had been running from something. Someone. And whatever he'd done, it had been enough to get him killed.

At six o'clock, I flipped the sign to Closed and locked the front door. Lily and I cleaned up in silence, both of us lost in our own thoughts.

"I should have turned the laptop over to Iris," I said finally. "When she came to tell me about the murder. I should have given it to her then."

"Why didn't you?"

I thought about it. About my instincts, my reasons. "Because Grant gave it to me. Trusted me with it. And because..." I hesitated. "Because something told me there was more to this than a simple theft. And I wanted to understand what we were dealing with before we handed it over to people who might not understand."

"Or people who might not be able to crack the password."

"That too." I pulled the laptop from its hiding spot, weighing it in my hands. "Maybe Maeve can help us figure out how to get into this. She helped us with Warren's computer at the library."

"It's worth asking," Lily agreed.

After dark, we slipped out the back door with the laptop hidden in a messenger bag. The streets were quiet, the shops closed, only a few lights burning in apartment windows above the storefronts. We took the long way to Maeve's, cutting through alleys and side streets, our breath misting in the cold air.

We were halfway down Birch Street when I felt it.

A prickle at the back of my neck. A sensation of being watched that had nothing to do with the murder or the mysterious man asking questions around town. This was different. Older. More familiar, in a way that made my stomach clench with something close to recognition.

I stopped walking, scanning the shadows between buildings. The street was empty. No movement, no sound except the distant hum of a car on the main road.

"Alexis?" Lily had stopped too, her hand on my arm. "What is it?"

"I don't know. I just..." I shook my head. "Did you feel anything? Just now?"

She was quiet for a moment, her eyes going slightly unfocused the way they did when she was reading the energy around us. "There's something. Faint. Like an echo of magic, but distant. Watching."

"That's what Poppy said this morning. That something was watching."

"It doesn't feel connected to the murder. This is something else."

The sensation faded as quickly as it had come, leaving me with nothing but a lingering unease and a memory I couldn't quite place. Something from my past, from the life I'd left behind. Something that whispered of the coven I'd fled nearly two years ago.

But that was impossible. They couldn't have found me. Not after all this time. Not here, in this quiet mountain town where I'd finally started to feel safe.

"Let's keep moving," I said, pushing the feeling aside. "We can worry about mysterious watchers later. Right now, we need to get this laptop to Maeve."

But as we continued down the dark street, I couldn't shake the sense that something had shifted. That the careful anonymity I'd built over the past year was starting to crack.

And that whatever was watching us wasn't going to stop.

Maeve was waiting at the side door, as if she'd known we were coming. She probably had.

"Trouble follows that machine," she said, taking the bag from me. "I've felt it since he first brought it into your café. Whatever secrets it holds, they're heavy ones."

"Can you keep it safe?"

"I can keep it hidden. And warded. Nothing with ill intent will find it here." She looked at both of us with those ancient eyes. "But eventually, you'll need to open it. Discover what's inside. And then the real danger begins."

"That's actually something we wanted to ask you about," I said. "I tried opening it before we left, but it was password protected. So, Lily and I were thinking about the psychometry spell we did at the library. With Warren's computer. Do you think we could do something similar here? To figure out the password?"

Maeve considered this, turning the laptop over in her hands. "The spell we used before was designed to reveal what had already been displayed. Search histories, documents, images. This is different. You're trying to discover something that was never shown on the screen at all."

"So, it won't work?" Lily asked.

"I didn't say that." Maeve's eyes took on that distant look they got when she was thinking through magical possibilities. "The password exists as a pattern. A sequence of keys pressed in a specific order, over and over again. That kind of repetition leaves traces. Emotional residue on the keys themselves."

"So instead of reading what the computer showed, we'd be reading what his fingers touched," I said slowly. "Which keys he pressed most often. What he was feeling when he typed them."

"Exactly. It's a variation on the same principle, but focused differently." Maeve set the laptop on her counter. "I'll need to do some research. Adapt the spell for this purpose. It's not something I've attempted before, but the theory is sound."

"How long do you need?"

"Give me a day or two. I want to do this right." She fixed us both with a serious look. "In the meantime, be careful. Whoever killed Grant is still out there, still looking for whatever he hid. And they won't stop just because the laptop is safely warded."

"We know," Lily said.

"Do you?" Maeve's voice was gentle but serious. "A man died for what's on that machine. Others may be willing to kill for it too. Are you prepared for that?"

I thought about Grant's nervous eyes. About Dina's bitter anger. About dangerous people who don't stop looking until they find what they're owed. About the watching man with his forgettable face and his patient surveillance.

And about that other feeling, the one that had nothing to do with the murder. The sense of being watched by something older, something that knew me.

"I don't know," I admitted. "But I know I can't ignore it. Whatever Grant was hiding, it got him killed. And if there's a chance it can help catch his killer..."

"Then you have to try." Maeve nodded. "I understand. Just promise me you'll be careful. Both of you. Magic can protect against many things, but it can't stop a bullet."

We promised. And we meant it.

But as Lily and I walked home through the quiet streets, I couldn't shake the feeling that careful might not be enough. That whatever Grant Granger had gotten himself into, we were now part of it too.

Whether we wanted to be or not.

And somewhere in the darkness behind us, something was still watching.

Waiting.

Patient as stone.

## Chapter Five

We were halfway back to the café when Lily stopped walking.
"What time is it?"

I checked my phone. "Just after seven. Why?"

"Didn't Lionel invite you to game night? Friday nights at his
shop?"

I'd completely forgotten. With everything that had happened,
Grant's murder and Dina's arrival and the laptop and Maeve's
ominous warnings, game night had slipped entirely from my mind.

"I don't know if I'm up for it," I admitted. "It's been a long day.
And after what we just felt back there..." I glanced over my shoulder,
but the street behind us was empty. No sign of whatever had been
watching us. No sign of anything at all.

"All the more reason to go." Lily linked her arm through mine.
"You need something normal. Something that isn't murder and
mystery and password-protected secrets. Besides, I could use a
distraction too."

She had a point. And Lionel had specifically invited me. It
would be rude not to at least stop by.

"Fine. But just for an hour or two."

The Rebel Rogue was only a few doors down from the café, so
we were already heading the right direction. The night was cold but
clear now, the earlier sense of being watched fading with each step.
Maybe I'd imagined it. Maybe it was just nerves, the weight of
everything that had happened catching up with me.

Or maybe something really was out there, and it had simply
decided to wait.

I pushed the thought aside. Tonight, I was going to be normal.
I was going to play games with friends and drink tea and pretend that
my life wasn't tangled up in murder and magic and secrets I couldn't
share.

Lionel's comic shop was warm and bright when we arrived.
The front section was dedicated to retail, rows of comics and graphic
novels and collectibles arranged with obvious care. Vintage posters
lined the walls, and a display case near the register held what looked
like signed first editions. The whole place smelled like paper and ink
and something warm, maybe cinnamon, drifting from the back.

The back of the shop had been converted into a gaming space with several large tables and comfortable chairs. Mismatched lamps created pools of warm light, and bookshelves stuffed with board games lined the walls. A handful of people were already gathered around one of the tables, setting up what looked like a complicated board game with dozens of tiny pieces.

Lionel looked up when the door chimed, and his face broke into a genuine smile. "Alexis! Lily! You made it."

"We almost didn't," I admitted. "It's been quite a day."

"I heard. The whole town's been talking about nothing else." He came around the counter and gestured toward the back. "Come on, we're just getting started. Esther brought her new cooperative game, the one about building a haunted mansion."

As we passed the small beverage station he'd set up, I noticed he'd already put out a pot of the lavender chamomile blend I'd mentioned liking once, weeks ago. Just one comment, made in passing, and he'd remembered.

"Help yourself," he said, noticing my glance. "I thought you might stop by, so I brewed some of your favorite."

"You remembered."

"Of course." He said it simply, like it wasn't anything special. Like remembering small details about people was just what you did.

I poured myself a cup, the familiar scent already easing some of the tension in my shoulders.

The group at the table included Esther James, the high school English teacher with sharp eyes and graying hair pulled back in her usual ponytail. She was arranging game tiles with the precision of someone who'd read the rulebook three times. Gabe from the hardware store was there too, quiet and careful as always, his large hands surprisingly gentle with the delicate game pieces. Rory, the youngest of the group, was practically vibrating with enthusiasm, his freckles standing out against his pale skin as he examined the game board. There was also a couple I recognized from the café, Clementine and her husband Felix, who ran the antique shop on Birch Street.

"Alexis!" Esther waved us over. "Perfect timing. We needed two more players to make the game work properly."

"What are we playing?" Lily asked, settling into a chair.

"Haunted Halls," Esther said, launching into an explanation with obvious relish. "It's cooperative, which means we're all working together against the game itself. We're building a haunted mansion, room by room, but there are ghosts trying to stop us. Each player has a special ability, and we have to use them strategically to complete the mansion before midnight strikes."

"Midnight being the game clock," Rory clarified. "Every round, the clock advances. If we don't finish before twelve..."

"We all lose," Esther finished. "Together. Which is why communication and planning are essential."

I chose the character card for the Medium, whose special ability was sensing where ghosts would appear next. It seemed fitting, given my actual abilities. Lily took the Architect, who could build rooms faster than anyone else.

We settled into chairs, and Esther walked us through the mechanics. Something about constructing rooms, avoiding ghosts, and working together to complete the mansion before the clock ran out. I tried to focus, but my mind kept drifting back to laptops and passwords and dangerous people who send others to do their dirty work.

"You okay?" Lionel asked quietly, leaning close while Esther demonstrated a game mechanic to Lily.

"Just tired. It's been a strange few days."

"I can imagine. Finding out one of your regulars was murdered..." He shook his head. "That can't be easy."

"It isn't. And it keeps getting more complicated."

He didn't press for details, just nodded with understanding. "Well, you're welcome to stay as long as you like. Or leave whenever you need to. No pressure."

It was such a simple thing to say. No pressure. But something about the way he said it, calm and genuine, made me feel like I could actually breathe for the first time all day.

He smiled and turned back to the game, shifting down to give Rory more room at the table. He was now seated across from me at the table.

The door chimed again, and I looked up to see Colton walking in.

He spotted me almost immediately, his face lighting up with surprise and pleasure. "Alexis! I didn't expect to see you here."

"Last minute decision," I said as he pulled up a chair beside me. Not across from me, or in any of the other empty seats. Right beside me, close enough that his shoulder brushed mine. "Lily convinced me I needed a break from everything."

"Smart thinking." He placed his hand over mine on the table, a brief, warm touch. "You've been through a lot this week. I'm glad you're here."

"Do you know how to play?" Esther asked, eyeing him with the mild suspicion of someone whose carefully balanced player count had just been disrupted.

"I'll figure it out as we go," Colton said confidently. "I'm a quick learner."

Across the table, I caught Lionel watching us. His expression didn't change, remained friendly and open, but something flickered in his eyes before he turned back to help Gabe with his game pieces.

The game began, and for a while, I managed to lose myself in the mechanics of building haunted rooms and dodging spectral threats. My Medium ability proved useful, letting me warn the group before ghosts appeared in newly constructed rooms.

"Ghost in the ballroom next round," I announced. "We should reinforce the east wing before building there."

"Good catch," Esther said approvingly. "Rory, use your Banisher ability to clear the corridor first."

"On it!"

There was something satisfying about the teamwork, the way everyone's abilities complemented each other. Even Colton, despite his late arrival, picked up the mechanics quickly and started contributing useful suggestions.

"If we build the library here," he said, pointing to a spot on the board, "it connects to both the study and the conservatory. More efficient."

"That's actually smart," Rory admitted.

But as the game progressed, I noticed Colton had started making decisions without consulting the group. Moving pieces before discussion was finished. Redirecting strategy based on what he thought was best.

"We should build the tower next," he announced during round six.

"Actually," Lily said, "I think the kitchen would be more strategic. It has a lower ghost risk."

"The tower gives us more points. Trust me, it's the better move."

He built the tower before anyone could object.

It wasn't wrong, exactly. The tower did give us more points. But it wasn't how cooperative games were supposed to work. You discussed. You reached consensus. You didn't just decide for everyone.

I caught Lily's eye across the table. She raised an eyebrow almost imperceptibly.

But the conversation kept drifting back to the murder, as conversations in small towns always do.

"I heard he wasn't even a real travel writer," Clementine said as she placed a corridor tile. "Mildred at the post office said he was receiving mail under three different names."

"Three names?" Felix raised his eyebrows. "That's suspicious."

"More than suspicious," Esther said. "That's criminal behavior. Mail fraud, at minimum."

I'd heard this same gossip at the café this morning, almost word for word. Small towns had a way of circulating information until everyone had heard the same story from six different sources, each one convinced they were sharing something new.

"Did anyone actually see anything that day?" Lily asked. "The day he went up to the falls?"

"Old Vernon Holt was up that way," Gabe said, his deep voice thoughtful. "I ran into him at the hardware store yesterday. He was buying new locks for his cabin. Heavy-duty deadbolts, the kind you use when you're worried about break-ins."

My ears perked up. "Vernon Holt?"

"Lives up in the hills, past the falls. Been there for twenty years or more." Gabe shrugged his massive shoulders. "Keeps to himself mostly. But he seemed agitated. More than usual, I mean. Vernon's always been a bit wound up, but this was different."

"Different how?" I pressed.

"Jumpy. Kept looking over his shoulder while we talked. And he mentioned something about trespassers on his property. Said he'd seen that writer fellow poking around where he shouldn't be." Gabe paused. "Said if he caught anyone else on his land, they'd regret it."

Lily and I exchanged a glance. Grant poking around on someone's property? That didn't sound like research for a travel book.

"Vernon's always been territorial," Esther said, though her tone was less dismissive than before. "Remember when he threatened to shoot Jasper's dog for wandering onto his land?"

"He never actually shot the dog," Rory pointed out.

"That's not the point. The point is he's volatile." Esther placed a ghost token on the board with more force than necessary. "I taught his nephew years ago. Sweet kid, but terrified of his uncle. Said Vernon had a room in his cabin he wasn't allowed to enter. Kept it locked at all times."

"A locked room?" Clementine leaned forward. "That's suspicious."

"It's probably just storage," Felix said. "Old hunting equipment or something."

"Or something he doesn't want anyone to see." Esther's eyes gleamed with the particular light of someone who'd read too many mystery novels. "I wouldn't be surprised if he finally snapped."

"Has anyone seen that woman claiming to be Grant's ex?" Clementine asked, lowering her voice slightly. "Blonde, intense looking? She was at the Pine Lodge this morning making all kinds of accusations."

"I heard she went to the sheriff's station and caused quite a scene," Felix added. "Said Grant stole money from her. A lot of money."

I kept my expression neutral, not wanting to reveal that Dina had come to the café. "Did anyone hear how much?"

"Forty thousand, according to Mildred." Clementine shook her head. "Can you imagine? I'd want to kill someone too if they stole forty thousand dollars from me."

"Clementine!" Felix looked scandalized.

"I'm just saying. That's motive, isn't it?"

"Now, now," Colton interjected, his voice taking on that reasonable tone that somehow managed to sound like he was settling an argument. "Let's not go accusing people without evidence. Vernon's eccentric, but that doesn't make him a murderer. And this woman, whoever she is, just lost someone she was involved with. We shouldn't be spreading rumors about her either."

"Colton's right," Lionel agreed. "We should let the sheriff handle the investigation. Spreading rumors won't help anyone."

They'd said almost the same thing, but somehow Colton's version felt like a pronouncement while Lionel's felt like a suggestion. I filed the observation away without examining it too closely.

But I made a mental note. Vernon Holt, territorial and volatile, with a locked room in his cabin and a temper that scared his own family. Another name to add to the list of people who might have wanted Grant dead.

As the game continued, I happened to glance toward the front window. A figure was standing outside, across the street, half-hidden in the shadow of a doorway.

Forgettable build. Forgettable posture. The kind of person your eyes would slide right past if you weren't looking for them.

The watching man.

My breath caught. He was just standing there, motionless, his attention fixed on the comic shop. On us.

"Alexis?" Lily touched my arm. "What is it?"

I looked back at the window. The doorway was empty. The street was quiet. No sign of anyone at all.

"Nothing," I said slowly. "I thought I saw... nothing. It's nothing."

But my heart was pounding, and the warmth of the evening had suddenly gone cold.

Lily caught my eye, a question in her gaze. I shook my head slightly. Later.

The game wrapped up a few minutes later, our team completing the mansion with two rounds to spare. Rory cheered, Esther looked satisfied, and even Gabe cracked a rare smile. But I couldn't shake the chill that had settled over me, and when Lily stifled a yawn, I seized the excuse.

"I think we should head out," I said. "It's been a long day."

"Good teamwork tonight," Lionel said. "Same time next week?"

"Wouldn't miss it," Esther replied, already packing up the game with careful precision.

"Thank you for having us," I told Lionel as we gathered our coats. "This was exactly what I needed."

"Anytime. You're always welcome here." He smiled, and there was something in his eyes, patient and steady. "Take care of yourself, Alexis."

He didn't try to walk me to the door. Didn't ask when he'd see me again. Just offered warmth without expectation and let me choose what to do with it.

Colton walked us to the door. "I'll call you tomorrow about dinner," he said, squeezing my hand. "Maybe we can try that Italian place in Silverpine again? I already know what I want to order for us."

For us. Not what he wanted to order for himself. For us.

"That sounds nice," I said, because I didn't know what else to say.

He leaned in and kissed my cheek, lingering just a moment longer than necessary. His hand rested on my lower back, warm and proprietary. "Goodnight, Alexis."

As Lily and I stepped out into the cold night air, I felt it again. That prickle at the back of my neck. That sense of being watched by something that had nothing to do with forgettable men or murder investigations.

I scanned the street. Empty. Quiet. Just snowbanks and closed shops and the distant glow of streetlights.

But the feeling persisted, a whisper of something ancient and patient. Something that knew me.

"Do you feel that?" I murmured to Lily.

She was quiet for a moment, her breath misting in the cold air. "Yes. It's fainter here, but it's the same thing we felt earlier. Near Maeve's."

"What do you think it is?"

"I don't know. But it's magical. Old magic." She glanced at me. "It could be the ley lines. This town sits on a convergence. Sometimes the energy gets... attentive."

"Attentive," I repeated. "That's a comforting way to put it."

"Would you prefer 'watchful?' 'Interested?' 'Focused on us specifically?'"

"No. Attentive is fine."

We walked in silence for a while, both of us lost in thought. The feeling faded as we moved, but it didn't disappear entirely. Just settled into the background, a low hum of awareness that hadn't been there a week ago.

"So," Lily said finally. "Interesting evening."

"You mean the murder gossip or the ghost game?"

"I mean watching those two circle you like cats around a food bowl."

I sighed. "They're not circling me."

"Colton put his hand on you fourteen times tonight. I counted."

"You counted?"

"I was curious." She shrugged. "Fourteen times. Hand on your shoulder, hand on your back, hand over yours on the table, knee against yours under it. He's marking territory."

"That's not..." I trailed off, because I couldn't actually finish the sentence. "He's just affectionate."

"He's affectionate in a very specific direction." Lily linked her arm through mine. "I'm not saying it's bad. He clearly likes you. He's handsome, successful, kind. There's nothing wrong with him."

"But?"

"But Lionel likes you too. And he's not trying to prove anything to anyone. He remembered your favorite tea. He gave you space to breathe. When you said you'd been through a lot, he didn't ask questions, he just... accepted it." She glanced at me. "Different approaches. That's all I'm saying."

"Colton's approach isn't wrong."

"I didn't say it was wrong. I said it was different." She paused. "The question is which approach makes you feel more like yourself."

I didn't have a response to that. So, I just kept walking, turning her words over in my mind.

Two men. Two approaches. And me, caught somewhere in the middle, not sure what I wanted or who I wanted it with.

The feeling of being watched had faded entirely by the time we reached the café. Lily squeezed my arm before heading home, and I climbed the stairs to find the cats waiting at the top of the stairs, Gus looking annoyed at our late return, Poppy radiating calm concern.

"You were gone a long time," Gus said. "I was worried. Also, hungry."

"You have food in your bowl."

"I was emotionally hungry."

I scooped him up and held him close, burying my face in his fur. "I'm sorry. It's been a complicated day."

"Most of your days are complicated lately," Poppy observed. "You should have more simple days. Simple days are better for napping."

"I'll work on that."

But as I got ready for bed, Lily's question kept echoing in my mind. *Which approach makes you feel more like yourself?*

Colton made me feel wanted. Pursued. Like something worth claiming.

Lionel made me feel... seen. Accepted. Like I didn't have to be anything other than what I already was.

Both were appealing in different ways. Both came with their own complications.

But that was a problem for another day. Tonight, I just wanted to curl up with my cats and try not to think about murder or mystery or the complications of the heart.

Or the something out there in the darkness that was watching. Waiting. Patient as stone.

Tomorrow would be soon enough for all of that.

# Chapter Six

Saturday brought more snow and more gossip. The café was busy from the moment I opened the doors, filled with locals hungry for news and tourists hungry for the morbid thrill of visiting a murder town. I hated that phrase, murder town, but I'd already heard it three times before noon.

"Word's spreading," Lily observed during a brief lull. "People are coming from Silverpine and Millbrook just to rubberneck."

"Let them. At least they're buying coffee."

But the attention made me uneasy. Every unfamiliar face could be a curious tourist or something more dangerous. I found myself watching the door, cataloging each new arrival, waiting for someone who didn't fit the pattern.

Flo came by around nine with her morning delivery, boxes of pastries balanced in her arms. She was a fixture in Larkspur Valley, had been running her bakery for thirty years, and knew everyone's business whether they wanted her to or not.

"Busy morning?" I asked, helping her unload.

"You have no idea. Everyone wants to talk about the murder." She lowered her voice. "Had a strange one in the diner yesterday, though. Man sitting by himself, nursing a single cup of coffee for two hours. Barely touched it. Just sat there watching the street."

My attention sharpened. "What did he look like?"

"That's the thing. I couldn't really tell you. Medium everything. Brown hair, going gray. The kind of face you forget the second you look away." She shook her head. "Gave me the creeps, honestly. When Hattie asked for his name for the check, he said Martin. Martin Oakes. Paid in cash and left without a word."

Martin Oakes. Finally, a name for the watching man.

"Did he say what he was doing in town?"

"Didn't say much of anything. Just watched." Flo arranged the pastries in the display case with practiced efficiency. "I mentioned it to Iris when she came in for breakfast. She said she'd look into it, but you know how stretched thin she is right now."

After Flo left, I pulled Lily aside. "Martin Oakes. That's the man who's been watching the café."

"The watcher? The one with the unremarkable face? You're sure?"

"Flo's description matches perfectly. And he was at her diner doing the same thing he's been doing here. Watching. Waiting."

"For what?"

"I don't know. But I don't think it's a coincidence that he showed up right around the time Grant was killed."

Dina Marsh came in around ten, ordered a black coffee, and settled into the corner with her phone and a notebook. She acknowledged me with a brief nod but didn't approach the counter again. Working on her own investigation, I assumed.

Sheriff Iris stopped by at eleven, ordering her usual coffee to go. She looked tired, dark circles under her eyes suggesting she hadn't slept much either. Her gaze swept the café as I made her drink, and I saw her clock Dina in the corner.

"Making progress?" I asked, keeping my voice low as I handed her the cup.

Iris leaned in, matching my volume. "Some. Grant had a record in three states. Fraud, mostly. Small-time stuff until about two years ago, when he seems to have graduated to bigger targets." She glanced toward Dina's corner. "That one's been cooperative, at least. Gave us everything she had on Grant. She's one of at least six women he conned. We're still trying to track down the others."

"Any of them angry enough to kill him?"

"All of them, probably. But angry enough to travel to a remote mountain town in winter to do it?" She shrugged. "That's what I'm trying to figure out."

"What about Vernon Holt? I heard he had a confrontation with Grant on the trails."

Iris's expression tightened slightly. "I've talked to Vernon. He admits he confronted Grant about trespassing, says he told him to stay off his property. Claims he went home after that and didn't see Grant again."

"Do you believe him?"

"Vernon's got a temper, and he's protective of his land. But he's also lived here for twenty years without killing anyone." She paused. "That said, he doesn't have anyone who can verify his whereabouts for the rest of that day. He lives alone, doesn't have neighbors close enough to notice his comings and goings."

"So, he's still a suspect."

"Everyone's still a suspect until I have evidence saying otherwise." She took a sip of her coffee. "Flo mentioned a man named Martin Oakes. Said you might have seen him too?"

"He's been watching the café. Tuesday he stood outside looking in. Wednesday he came inside, sat for an hour, barely touched his drink. I saw him again last night outside Lionel's shop."

"Description?"

"That's the thing. His features are completely unremarkable. Medium height, medium build, brown hair going gray. The kind of face your eyes slide right past." I paused. "But the way he behaves makes him impossible to ignore. Sitting for hours without really doing anything, just watching. If he acted normal, no one would remember him at all. But he doesn't act normal."

Iris nodded slowly. "So, he's trying to blend in, but he's bad at it."

"Or he doesn't care if people notice him watching. Which might be worse."

Iris made a note. "I'll see what I can find. Might be nothing, might be something." She tucked her notebook away. "If you think of anything else, you know where to find me."

After she left, I noticed Dina watching from her corner table. When our eyes met, she raised her coffee cup in a small salute. A fellow investigator, that gesture seemed to say. We're on the same side.

I wasn't sure I agreed with that assessment. But I nodded back anyway.

My phone buzzed with a text from Colton: "Still on for tonight? I made reservations at Bellini's for 7. Can't wait to see you."

I typed back: "Looking forward to it."

"Hot date tonight?" Lily asked, appearing at my elbow.

"Second date. The Italian place in Silverpine."

"The one where he ordered for you?"

I shot her a look. "He was being thoughtful."

"I didn't say anything." But her expression said plenty.

Around noon, Dina packed up her things and stopped at the counter on her way out.

"I'm going to do some digging around town," she said. "See if anyone else remembers anything useful about Grant. I'll be at the lodge if you hear anything."

"I'll let you know."

She gave me a long look, like she was still trying to decide whether to trust me. Then she nodded and left.

The lunch rush kept us busy until two o'clock. Then the café emptied out, the way it often did on Saturday afternoons. Locals went home for chores and family time. Tourists headed to the hiking trails or the ski slopes in the next valley over.

I was restocking the pastry case when the door chimed.

The man who walked in was different from Martin Oakes, though something about him raised the same alarm bells. Mid-forties, taller and broader, with sharp features and eyes that assessed the room with cold efficiency. He wore an expensive jacket that didn't quite fit the mountain town aesthetic, and his smile, when he offered it, didn't reach his eyes.

Rocky, who had been dozing on his favorite shelf, suddenly lifted his head. His orange fur bristled slightly, and a low growl rumbled in his throat.

That caught my attention. Rocky didn't growl. Rocky was chaos and energy and friendliness. Rocky loved everyone.

The man approached the counter with an easy smile that didn't quite reach his eyes. "Good afternoon. I'm looking for some information, and I was told this might be a good place to start."

Rocky's growl grew louder. Across the room, Gus had gone very still on his perch, watching the newcomer with unusual intensity. Poppy had positioned herself near the cat room door, her body language subtly protective. Even Millie had emerged slightly from behind her fern, her blue eyes fixed on the man.

Only Sage seemed oblivious, still napping in a patch of sunlight by the window.

"What kind of information are you looking for?" I asked, keeping my voice neutral.

"My friend Grant Granger." He moved closer to the counter, his movements smooth and controlled. Almost too controlled, like someone who was very aware of how he appeared to others. "We were supposed to meet up a few days ago, but I haven't been able to reach him. His phone goes straight to voicemail. I'm getting worried."

Rocky hissed, loud and sharp.

The man glanced at him, and for just a moment, his pleasant mask slipped. Something cold flickered in his eyes before the smile returned.

"Friendly cat."

"He's usually very sweet," I said. "He must be having an off day. I'm sorry, I didn't catch your name."

"Albert. Albert Crane." He extended his hand across the counter. I took it briefly, resisting the urge to wipe my palm on my apron afterward. His grip was firm but cold.

"I'm Alexis. This is my café."

"It's charming." His eyes swept the room, cataloging everything. The few remaining customers. The exits. The back room door. "Very cozy. I can see why Grant liked it here."

"You knew Grant well?"

"College roommates. We've stayed in touch over the years, met up whenever our paths crossed." He shook his head sadly. "I've been traveling and just arrived in town yesterday. I came straight here hoping someone might know where to find him."

"I'm sorry to tell you that Grant passed away," I said, watching his reaction carefully. "He was found at Aspen Falls. The sheriff is investigating."

The man's expression flickered. Just for a moment, just a fraction of a second, something passed through his eyes. Not grief. Not shock. Something calculating, quickly suppressed.

"Dead?" His voice carried exactly the right amount of disbelief. "No. That can't be right. I just talked to him last week."

"I'm sorry for your loss."

"This is terrible. Grant was a good friend." He pressed a hand to his chest, the gesture somehow wrong. Too practiced. Too perfect. "Do they know what happened? An accident on the trails?"

"The sheriff believes it was murder."

Something shifted in his expression. Interest, maybe. Or satisfaction. Gone before I could be sure.

"Murder? In a town like this?" He looked around with exaggerated surprise. "That's terrible. Do they have any suspects?"

"I wouldn't know. The sheriff is handling the investigation."

"Of course. Of course." He pulled out a small notepad and pen. "I'd like to leave my contact information. In case anyone remembers anything about Grant. Where he was staying, what he was doing. Any little detail could help me understand what happened to my friend."

I took the slip of paper he offered, glancing at the phone number scrawled across it. "I'll pass this along to the sheriff."

"I'd appreciate that. I'd be happy to speak with her as well. Anything to help bring closure to this terrible situation." He tucked his notepad away, his movements precise and economical. "One more thing. Do you know if Grant had his things with him? A bag, maybe? He was never without his laptop. Carried it everywhere."

The question was casual. Too casual.

"I wouldn't know," I said. "The sheriff would have more information about what was found at the scene."

"Of course." He smiled again, that empty smile that never touched his eyes. "Thank you for your time, Alexis. I'm sure I'll be around. Such a charming town. I think I might stay a few days, help out with the investigation however I can."

"That's very dedicated of you."

"Grant was my friend. The least I can do is make sure whoever did this is brought to justice." He headed for the door, then paused, looking back at me. "I hope your cat feels better soon. Animals can sense things, you know. They're very intuitive."

The bell chimed as he left, and I watched him walk down Main Street until he disappeared around a corner. Only then did I release the breath I'd been holding.

Rocky jumped down from his shelf and wound around my ankles, still bristling slightly. "Bad," he said. "That one is bad. Wrong. Don't trust."

"I know, Rocky."

Gus appeared at my other side. "His eyes were cold. Like a snake watching a mouse."

Poppy joined them, her tail still slightly puffed. "He was lying. About everything. The words were right, but the feeling underneath was all wrong."

"I know," I said again. "I felt it too."

Lily emerged from the back room where she'd been doing inventory during the lull.

"I heard most of that," she said quietly. "And I saw him when he walked in. His aura..." She shuddered. "Violence. Layers and layers of it, barely contained beneath the surface. And rage. Cold rage, the kind that doesn't burn out."

"Worse than Warren?"

"Different. Warren was desperate, unraveling. This man is controlled. Patient." She hugged herself. "Whatever he's feeling, it's not grief. He didn't care about Grant at all. He's here for something else."

"He asked about Grant's belongings. His bag. His laptop. Tried to make it sound like an afterthought."

"Which is at Maeve's. Safe."

"But he doesn't know that." I thought about Albert's questions, his careful interest. "He thinks it might still be out there somewhere. And if he figures out Grant spent a lot of time here..."

"He'll come looking."

"There's something else," I said slowly. "He claimed to be Grant's college roommate. But at game night last night, people were talking about Grant receiving mail under different names. If he was running cons for years, using fake identities..." I trailed off, thinking. "Would a real college roommate even know him as Grant Granger?"

"You think he's lying about knowing Grant?"

"I think he's lying about something. I just don't know what yet."

"And then there's Martin Oakes," Lily said. "The watcher. Two different men, both circling around Grant's death."

"Connected?"

"Maybe. Or maybe Grant made enough enemies that they're tripping over each other trying to find whatever he was hiding."

The door chimed, and we both jumped. But it was only Atticus Monroe, looking windswept and tired.

"Afternoon," he said, approaching the counter. "Black coffee, please."

I made his drink while he stood in uncomfortable silence. He looked like he wanted to say something but couldn't find the words.

"How are you doing?" I asked, handing him the coffee. "After everything?"

"I'm... managing." He wrapped both hands around the cup, as if seeking warmth. "I've been having strange dreams. And when I'm out on the trails, the animals..." He trailed off, shaking his head. "Never mind. You'll think I'm crazy."

"I won't. I promise."

He looked at me for a long moment, something searching in his expression. "Maeve said I could talk to you. That you'd understand. But I'm not sure I understand myself yet. What's happening to me."

"When you're ready," I said gently. "I'm here. And so is Maeve. And Lily. You're not as alone in this as you think."

Something flickered in his eyes. Relief, maybe. Or the first faint stirring of hope.

"Maybe tomorrow," he said. "I need to process a few more things first. But... thank you. For not thinking I'm losing my mind."

"You're not. I promise you're not."

He took his coffee to a corner table and sat staring out the window at the mountains. Whatever was happening inside him, whatever doors were opening, he wasn't ready to walk through them yet. But he would be. Soon.

The rest of the afternoon passed quietly. Too quietly, after the tension of Albert's visit. I kept expecting him to return, to ask more questions, to somehow know that the laptop he was looking for had passed through my hands.

But he didn't come back. Not that day.

At closing time, I locked the door and leaned against it, exhausted in a way that had nothing to do with the physical work of running a café.

"The cold man will be back," Poppy said from her perch. "He's not done searching."

"I know."

"And when he figures out you had the box with the buttons..."

"I know."

"What are you going to do?"

I thought about Albert Crane with his empty eyes and practiced smile. About Martin Oakes, the watcher, whose purpose remained unclear. About Atticus Monroe, teetering on the edge of a revelation that would change his life. About Vernon Holt with his temper and his secrets. About the laptop hidden at Maeve's, full of answers we hadn't yet uncovered.

"Tomorrow," I said. "We'll figure out something tomorrow."

But even as I said it, I knew tomorrow might not be soon enough. Albert was hunting. And whatever he was hunting for, he wouldn't stop until he found it.

Or until someone stopped him.

I checked the time. Just after six. Enough time to shower, change, and try to put on a normal face for my date with Colton.

"You're still going?" Lily asked, reading my expression.

"I need something normal tonight. Something that isn't murder and danger and men with cold eyes." I headed for the stairs. "Besides, I already said yes."

"Be careful," Lily said. "And have fun. You deserve a nice evening."

I wasn't sure I believed that. But I was going to try anyway.

## Chapter Seven

Saturday evening arrived with a gentle snowfall that made Larkspur Valley look like the inside of a snow globe. I stood in front of my closet, trying to decide what to wear and wondering why I was so nervous about a second date when I'd faced down murderers and solved crimes.

"You're overthinking," Poppy observed from her spot on my bed. "Just wear the green one. It's flattering."

"Since when do you know about fashion?"

"I know about colors. And I know you look confident in green. You stand taller when you wear it."

I pulled out the forest green blouse, soft and flowing, and paired it with black pants and ankle boots. I'd worn the blue sweater on our first date, and something about repeating the outfit felt wrong. Like I wasn't putting in effort.

"You're going out with the healing man again," Gus observed from his perch on the windowsill. "The one who smells like dog medicine and confidence."

"His name is Colton. And yes, we're having dinner."

"Will you be gone long? I don't like when you're gone long."

"A few hours. You'll survive."

Rocky bounded in, his orange fur slightly damp from what I suspected was an ill-advised encounter with the bathroom sink. "Are you nervous? You smell nervous. And also like that flower water."

"Perfume. It's called perfume."

"I like how you smell without it better. More like you."

"I'll keep that in mind."

There was a knock at my apartment door, and I opened it to find Lily with two mugs of tea.

"Thought you could use some calm before your date," she said, handing me one. "Chamomile with a touch of lavender."

"You're a lifesaver." I took a sip, feeling the warmth spread through me. "I don't know why I'm so nervous. It's just dinner."

"It's not just dinner. It's a second date, which means it's officially becoming something." She settled onto the arm of my couch, studying me with those perceptive eyes. "How are you feeling about that?"

"I don't know. Good, I think? Colton's wonderful. He's kind and successful and he actually seems to like me."

"But?"

"There's no but."

Lily raised an eyebrow in an expression remarkably similar to Poppy's. "There's always a but with you. You're the most complicated person I know, and I say that with love."

I sighed. "We're going to the same Italian place in Silverpine. When I suggested trying somewhere new, he said 'Why change what works?' with this warm smile, and I just... didn't push it."

"And that bothers you?"

"I don't know if it bothers me. It's practical. Sensible." I fiddled with my earring. "I just keep comparing him to Lionel. And I don't know why. Lionel and I aren't anything. We've never even been on a date."

"Maybe that's the point. Lionel represents possibility. The path not taken." She shrugged. "Colton is the path you're actually walking. That's scarier."

"When did you become so wise about relationships?"

"I'm not wise. I'm just observant." She stood, taking her mug with her. "Have fun tonight. And try to stay in the moment instead of analyzing everything."

"I'll try."

After she left, I finished getting ready. A touch of makeup, nothing too dramatic. Earrings that caught the light. A final check in the mirror to make sure everything was in place.

Colton was picking me up at six-thirty. Part of me wished we were trying somewhere new, but I pushed the thought aside. The restaurant was good. The company would be good. That was what mattered.

Colton arrived right on time, knocking on my apartment door at the top of the exterior staircase. He was wearing a charcoal gray sweater that made his hazel eyes stand out, and his smile when he saw me was genuine and warm.

"You look beautiful," he said.

"Thank you. You clean up pretty well yourself."

He offered his arm. "Shall we?"

The drive to Silverpine was comfortable, the conversation easy. He asked about the café, about how the investigation was affecting business, about whether I was holding up okay under the stress.

"It's been a lot," I admitted. "Another murder, more questions than answers. But I'm managing."

"You're stronger than you give yourself credit for." He reached over and squeezed my hand briefly before returning his attention to the snowy road. "I've seen how you handle pressure. You don't crack. You just... figure it out."

"Sometimes I feel like I'm barely holding it together."

"Everyone feels that way. The difference is what you do about it." He glanced at me with those warm hazel eyes. "You keep going. You take care of your cats, your customers, your friends. That's not nothing, Alexis. That's everything."

Something in my chest loosened at his words. It was nice to be seen that way. Nice to have someone notice the effort behind the composure.

The restaurant was warm and bustling, the Saturday evening crowd filling most of the tables. The hostess recognized Colton from our previous visit and led us to a quiet corner booth with a candle flickering between us.

"I come here more often than I should admit," Colton confessed as the hostess handed us menus. "There's something about the chicken piccata that I can't resist."

"You mentioned that last time. It was good."

"Good enough to order again?"

I'd been thinking about trying the seafood risotto this time, actually. Before I could respond, the waiter appeared.

"We'll have the bruschetta to start," Colton said with that confident smile. "And a bottle of the Montepulciano. The 2018 if you have it." He glanced at the menu, then at me. "And two chicken piccatas. It really is the best thing here."

"Actually," I said, before the waiter could leave, "may I have the seafood risotto instead?"

The waiter nodded and made a note.

Colton's smile flickered, just for a moment. A brief flash of something that might have been surprise, or might have been disappointment.

"I hope you don't mind," I said. "I just wanted to try something different this time."

"Of course not." His smile returned, warm and easy. "You should get what you want. I just thought since you loved the piccata so much last time..."

"I did. But variety is nice too."

"Absolutely." He nodded, but something in his expression suggested he was recalibrating. Adjusting to the idea that I might not always follow his lead.

The wine arrived, and Colton made a small production of tasting it, swirling, sniffing, nodding his approval. He poured for both of us and raised his glass.

"To us," he said. "And to wherever this is going."

"To us."

We clinked glasses, and the conversation flowed naturally. He told me about a difficult surgery he'd performed earlier that week, a golden retriever who'd swallowed a child's toy and needed emergency intervention.

"The toy was a rubber duck," he said, shaking his head. "Bright yellow, about two inches tall. The dog had swallowed it whole."

"Did the dog survive?"

"She's doing great. Already back to terrorizing her family." His eyes crinkled with affection. "That's the best part of this job. When you can give someone back their family member. Even the furry ones."

"You really love what you do."

"I do. I can't imagine doing anything else." He took a sip of wine, then set the glass down. "What about you? Did you always know you wanted to run a café?"

The question caught me off guard. My path to The Cozy Purrch had been anything but straightforward, tangled up with magic and running and a past I couldn't fully explain.

"Not always," I said carefully. "I tried a lot of different things before I found my way here. But once I landed in Larkspur Valley, it just felt right. Like I'd found the place I was supposed to be."

"I felt that way when I first moved here too. I was doing my residency in Denver, planning to stay there, build a practice in the city. Then I came up here for a weekend trip, and something just... clicked." He smiled. "Two weeks later, I was interviewing for the position at the animal hospital. Six months after that, I was a full partner."

"You don't miss the city?"

"Sometimes. The restaurants, the nightlife, the feeling that everything was happening all around you." He shrugged. "But I don't miss it enough to go back. There's something about the mountains. The quiet. The way everyone knows everyone else."

"That can be a curse as much as a blessing."

"True. You can't sneeze in this town without someone asking if you're coming down with something." He laughed. "But I'd rather have that than the anonymity of the city. Here, people actually care about each other."

It was then that I felt it.

A prickle at the back of my neck. That familiar sensation of being watched, of unseen eyes tracking my movements. I'd felt it before in Larkspur Valley and blamed the ley lines, the magical convergence that made the town's energy so attentive.

But we weren't in Larkspur Valley. We were in Silverpine, twenty miles away, well outside any convergence points I knew of.

This time, I didn't think it had anything to do with the ley lines.

I glanced around the restaurant, trying to be subtle about it. Couples enjoying dinner. A family with two young children. A group of women laughing over cocktails. Nothing out of place. No one watching.

But the feeling persisted. Something ancient and patient, something that knew me.

"Alexis?" Colton's voice cut through my thoughts. "Everything okay?"

"Fine." I forced a smile. "Just thought I saw someone I knew."

"Anyone interesting?"

"No. I was mistaken."

The feeling faded slowly, like a tide receding. But it left something behind, a residue of unease that settled in my chest and refused to dissolve.

Our entrees arrived. The seafood risotto was rich and creamy, studded with shrimp and scallops, and I was glad I'd spoken up.

"How is it?" Colton asked, watching me take my first bite.

"Delicious. Different from the piccata, but really good."

"I'm glad." He smiled, though I noticed he didn't ask to try it. "Sometimes trying something new works out."

"Sometimes it does."

He took a bite of his own meal, then set down his fork. "You know, I admire that about you. Knowing what you want and asking for it."

I paused, fork halfway to my mouth. Was that admiration in his voice, or something else? It was hard to tell.

"I don't always know what I want," I admitted. "But when I do, I try to say so."

"That's more than most people manage." His eyes twinkled. "Though I have to say, sometimes the safe choice is safe for a reason. That piccata never lets me down."

The safe choice. For some reason, the phrase stuck in my mind. Was Colton the safe choice? Steady, reliable, uncomplicated? And if he was, what did that make Lionel?

Lionel, who never assumed he knew what I wanted. Who asked instead of told. Who gave me space to choose for myself, even when that space sometimes felt like distance.

I shook off the thought. This wasn't the time to be comparing the two men in my life. I was on a date with Colton. A nice date. I should be present for it.

"You okay?" Colton asked, noticing my hesitation.

"Fine. Just savoring."

He smiled, accepting the deflection. "I've been thinking about something," he said, his tone shifting to something more serious. "About us."

"Oh?"

"I know it's only our second date. But I feel like there's something real here. Something worth pursuing." He reached across the table and took my hand. "I'd like to see where this goes. If you're willing."

"I'd like that too."

"Good." His thumb traced circles on the back of my hand. "I'm not interested in playing games, Alexis. I'm forty-two years old. I know what I want, and I go after it. Life's too short for uncertainty."

It was meant to be romantic. Decisive. The words of a man who knew his own mind and wasn't afraid to express it.

So why did something about it feel like a door closing?

Colton insisted on paying again, waving away my attempt to contribute.

"You paid last time too," I pointed out.

"And I'll pay next time. Consider it an investment in our future." He smiled. "Unless you'd like to cook for me sometime? I make a mean sous chef."

"I'll think about it." But even as I said it, something snagged in my mind. He'd offered to be my sous chef, which meant he was expecting me to cook for him. In my home. Without even asking if that was something I'd want. He hadn't meant it as anything other than a sweet gesture, I was sure of that. But it sat alongside all the other small things that didn't quite land right. Just like the paying without asking, the deciding for both of us, the certainty that what he wanted was also what I wanted.

He met my eyes across the table, his expression warm and certain. "I'm really glad we're doing this, Alexis. Getting to know each other. I feel like there's something real here."

"I feel that too." And I did. That was the complicated part. He was warm and attentive and easy to be around. I wanted this to work. I was trying to let it work. But somewhere beneath the pleasant evening and the good food and the genuine laughter, those small things kept surfacing, one after another, like stones turning up in a garden you thought you'd cleared.

The drive home was quiet but not awkwardly so. The snow had stopped, and the sky was clearing, stars beginning to appear between the clouds. I watched the dark shapes of mountains pass by the window, thinking about safe choices and closing doors and the feeling of being watched in a restaurant twenty miles from home.

Colton pulled up behind the café and put the car in park but didn't move to get out.

"I had a really nice time tonight," he said.

"Me too."

"Can I see you again next weekend? There's a new Thai place in Millbrook I've been wanting to try." He paused. "Unless you'd rather go somewhere else. I know I picked the last two restaurants."

The acknowledgment surprised me. Maybe he was more aware than I'd given him credit for.

"Thai sounds great," I said. "But maybe I can pick the place after that?"

"Deal." He smiled, warm and genuine. "I like a woman who knows what she wants."

He leaned over, his hand coming up to cup my cheek. The kiss was soft at first, gentle and questioning. I leaned into it, felt the warmth of his lips, the careful tenderness of his touch. When we pulled apart, he was smiling.

"Goodnight, Alexis."

"Goodnight, Colton."

I climbed the stairs to my apartment feeling lighter than I had in days, despite the lingering unease from that moment in the restaurant. The cats were waiting in their usual spots, watching me with knowing eyes as I hung up my coat and kicked off my boots.

"You smell happy," Sage announced, bouncing over to greet me. "And also, like bread and cheese."

"Italian food."

"Was the healing man nice to you?"

"He was very nice."

"Good." She rubbed against my ankles. "You deserve nice."

I scooped her up and carried her to the couch, where the others gradually joined us. Gus claimed his spot on the back of the couch. Rocky sprawled across my lap. Poppy curled up beside me, her warm weight comforting. Even Millie crept out from her hiding spot to sit at my feet.

"You're thinking loud thoughts," Poppy observed.

"Am I?"

"You always do, after you see the healing man. Thinking about whether you like him. Whether he likes you. Whether this is going somewhere."

"You're very perceptive for a cat."

"All cats are perceptive. Most humans just don't listen." She began to groom her paw. "Do you like him?"

I considered the question. Did I like Colton? He was handsome, kind, successful. He made me laugh. He saw something strong in me when I felt anything but. The kiss had been nice, warm and genuine.

"I think so," I said finally. "Yes. I like him."

"But?"

"There's no but."

Poppy paused her grooming to give me a long, steady look. "There's always a but. With you, especially. You never just feel one thing. You feel seventeen things all tangled together."

She wasn't wrong. Colton made me feel wanted, pursued, chosen. But he also made me feel... decided upon. Like he'd made up his mind about what he wanted, and I was part of that plan whether I'd agreed to it or not.

Was that a bad thing? To be wanted so clearly, so confidently? Most people would call that romantic.

So why did part of me keep thinking about Lionel, who never pushed, never assumed, never decided anything for me? Who just... waited. Patiently. Like he had all the time in the world.

"You're doing it again," Poppy said. "Thinking loud thoughts."

"Sorry."

"Don't apologize. Just try to sleep eventually. Tomorrow will have its own problems."

She wasn't wrong about that either.

I got ready for bed, trying to push the swirling thoughts aside. The date had been nice. Colton had been nice. The kiss had been nice. Nice was good. Nice was what I wanted.

Wasn't it?

As I lay in bed, waiting for sleep to come, my mind drifted back to that moment in the restaurant. The prickle at the back of my neck. The sense of being watched by something that had nothing to do with ley lines or magical convergences.

Something had found me. Or was finding me. Something that could reach me even outside Larkspur Valley's protective energy.

I'd been so focused on Grant's murder, on Albert Crane and Martin Oakes and whoever had pushed a con man off a cliff. But maybe there was another threat I'd been ignoring. A threat from my past, catching up to me at last.

Tomorrow, I would talk to Maeve. Ask her if she'd sensed anything. See if the wards around town were still holding.

But tonight, I would just try to sleep. Try to hold onto the warmth of a good date, a nice kiss, the possibility of something more.

Even if that something came with complications I wasn't ready to face.

# Chapter Eight

Sunday morning dawned bright and cold, the kind of winter day where the sun reflecting off the snow was almost blinding. I woke to Sage batting at my nose and Rocky sprawled across my chest like a furry orange weight.

"She's awake," Sage announced. "Finally."

"It's Sunday," I mumbled. "I'm allowed to sleep in."

"Someone is coming," Poppy said from her spot at the foot of the bed. "I can feel footsteps on the stairs."

I sat up, dislodging Rocky, who protested loudly. Footsteps on the exterior staircase meant someone was coming to my apartment door. On a Sunday morning, that was unusual.

I threw on a robe and padded to the door just as a tentative knock sounded.

Through the peephole, I saw Atticus Monroe, looking nervous and windswept.

I opened the door. "Atticus. Is everything okay?"

"I'm sorry to bother you at home. On a Sunday morning." He shifted his weight from foot to foot. "Maeve said you wouldn't mind, but if this is a bad time..."

"It's fine. Come in." I stepped aside to let him enter. "Can I make you some coffee?"

He nodded gratefully, and I led him into my small kitchen. The cats followed, curious about our visitor. Poppy watched from the doorway with knowing eyes. Gus positioned himself nearby, pretending to nap but clearly listening. Even Sage crept closer, her curiosity overcoming her usual shyness around strangers.

I started the coffee maker and leaned against the counter. "What's on your mind?"

Atticus stood awkwardly in my living room, taking in the space. The worn couch, the overflowing bookshelves, the cat trees strategically placed near the windows. "I couldn't sleep last night. Kept having dreams about flying. About seeing the world from above." He looked at me, his eyes searching. "Maeve said I could talk to you. That you'd understand."

"Sit down," I said gently. "Tell me everything."

He sank onto the couch, and for a long moment, just stared at his hands. "I've always had a connection with animals. Ever since I was a kid. I thought it was just... a knack. An intuition. But lately, it's been different. Stronger." He looked up at me. "The hawk. The one that led me to the falls. I didn't just see what it saw. I felt what it felt. The wind under its wings. The sharpness of its vision. And when it spotted the body..." He shuddered. "I felt its confusion. Its recognition that something was wrong."

"That must have been overwhelming."

"It was terrifying." He accepted the coffee I handed him, wrapping both hands around the mug. "I thought I was losing my mind. But Maeve said it was a gift. That I was finally waking up to something that had always been there."

"Maeve is usually right about these things."

"She said you have your own abilities." He said the word carefully, like he was testing it. "Is that true?"

I settled into the armchair across from him. "I can communicate with cats. Not just read their body language or guess what they're feeling. Actually hear them. Talk to them."

His eyes widened slightly, then flicked to the cats scattered around the room. Poppy met his gaze steadily. Gus pretended not to notice. Sage ducked behind a plant.

"They're all listening right now, aren't they?"

"They're curious about you. They can sense that you're changing."

"Changing." He laughed, but there was no humor in it. "That's one way to put it. I feel like I'm going crazy. Every time I go outside, I can feel the animals around me. The birds, the squirrels, the deer in the woods. It's like static in my head, all these fragments of sensation and emotion that aren't mine."

"It gets easier," I said. "You learn to filter it. To control when you're open and when you're closed."

"How long did it take you?"

I thought back to my own awakening, years ago in the coven. To the patient teachers who had helped me understand my gift. To the practice and discipline it had taken to master it.

"A while," I admitted. "But I had help. And so will you."

"Maeve offered to teach me. To help me understand what's happening." He met my eyes. "She said you and Lily might help too. That there are others in this town who are like us."

"There are. More than you might think." I smiled gently. "Larkspur Valley has a way of attracting people with gifts. Something about the land, the energy here."

"The ley lines," he said, surprising me. "Maeve mentioned those. Said the town sits on some kind of magical convergence."

"It does. It's part of why I ended up here." I hesitated, thinking about last night. The feeling of being watched in the restaurant in Silverpine, twenty miles away. "Though lately I've been feeling things that don't seem connected to the ley lines at all."

"What kind of things?"

"I'm not sure yet. Something I need to ask Maeve about." I shook my head. "But that's my problem, not yours. Tell me more about the hawk. What else did you see?"

"I've lived here my whole life. Born and raised." He shook his head slowly. "This is a lot to take in."

"It is. And you don't have to figure it all out today. Just know that you're not alone."

He was quiet for a moment, processing. Then he asked, "The body at the falls. Grant Granger. Do you think my gift led me there for a reason?"

"I don't know. Sometimes our gifts serve a larger purpose. Sometimes they're just there. But if you saw something through the hawk's eyes, something that might help find who did this..."

"I've been trying to remember." His brow furrowed. "The hawk noticed movement earlier that morning. Before the body was there. Someone on the trail, heading toward the falls. But it was just a shape, a blur of color. The hawk didn't care about humans unless they were a threat."

"What color?"

"Dark. Black or brown, maybe. A coat or jacket." He shook his head in frustration. "I'm sorry. It's not much."

"It's more than we had before." I reached over and touched his hand briefly. "Thank you for telling me. And for trusting me."

He managed a small smile. "Maeve said you were safe. The cats seem to agree."

As if on cue, Sage emerged from behind her plant and cautiously approached Atticus. She sniffed his shoe, then looked up at him with her wide, curious eyes.

"She says you smell like feathers and sky," I translated. "She thinks that's interesting."

Atticus laughed, and this time there was real warmth in it. "Tell her I think she's interesting too."

"You'll be able to tell her yourself, eventually. Once you learn to listen."

His expression shifted, something like wonder crossing his features. "You really think so?"

"I know so. You have a gift, Atticus. It's overwhelming right now, but it's also remarkable. Once you learn to control it, you'll be able to connect with animals in ways most people can't even imagine."

He nodded slowly, absorbing this. "I should let you get on with your day. But... thank you. For listening. For not making me feel crazy."

"Come by anytime. And keep talking to Maeve. She's been waiting a long time to help you with this."

After he left, I got dressed and checked my phone. A text from Lily: *Lunch at Rosemary's? Noon?*

Rosemary's Delicatessen was on the far end of Main Street, away from the café and the bookshop and all the places I usually frequented. It had been there for decades, run by the same family, serving the same sandwiches and homemade soups that had made it a Larkspur Valley institution.

*See you there*, I texted back.

I spent the rest of the morning tidying my apartment and trying not to think about the laptop hidden at Maeve's. About what secrets it might contain. About Albert Crane and his cold, searching eyes.

The walk to Rosemary's took me past the Pine Lodge, and I found myself scanning the parking lot for unfamiliar cars. Looking for signs of Albert or Dina or anyone else who might be hunting for Grant's secrets.

I was halfway down Main Street when I saw him.

Martin Oakes. Standing outside the general store, apparently studying the notices pinned to the community board. But his posture was wrong for casual reading. Too still. Too watchful. His eyes kept drifting toward the street, scanning the people walking past.

When his gaze swept over me, there was a brief flicker of interest. Recognition, maybe. He knew I ran the café where Grant had spent so much time. But it didn't feel personal. It felt like I was just another piece of a puzzle he was trying to solve.

He looked away, turning his attention back to the board.

I kept walking, forcing myself not to stare. Martin Oakes wasn't Albert Crane. He didn't radiate that cold menace, that barely contained violence. But there was something about his patient surveillance that unnerved me. He was watching this town, watching the places Grant had frequented.

What was he hoping to find?

Lily was already at a corner table when I arrived, a cup of soup steaming in front of her. "I ordered you the turkey and swiss," she said. "You mentioned the other day you were craving one. But I can flag down the waitress if you'd rather have something else."

The contrast hit me immediately. Colton ordering for me, confident he knew what I wanted. Lily ordering for me, but basing it on something I'd actually said, and still checking to make sure it was right.

"Turkey and swiss is perfect," I said, meaning it. I slid into the seat across from her. "Maeve called?"

"This morning. She's ready. Four o'clock."

"Good. I need to talk to her about something else too." I lowered my voice. "Last night, at dinner in Silverpine, I felt something. That prickling sensation, like being watched. But we were twenty miles outside of town."

Lily's expression sharpened. "Outside the ley line convergence."

"Exactly. Whatever it was, it wasn't the town's energy being 'attentive.' It was something else." I paused. "Something that could reach me even outside Larkspur Valley."

"The coven?"

The word hung between us, heavy with implication. I'd been running from them for nearly two years. Had convinced myself I was safe here, hidden in the magical fog of the convergence.

"I don't know. Maybe. Or maybe I'm being paranoid." I shook my head. "I'll ask Maeve if the wards are still holding. If anything's changed."

"We should tell her regardless. If something's watching you..."

"I know. I will."

The waitress brought my sandwich, and I forced myself to eat despite my churning stomach. After a few bites, I remembered my other news.

"Atticus came by my apartment earlier."

I filled her in on our conversation while we ate. The hawk vision, the dark figure on the trail, Atticus's growing acceptance of his gift.

"Another one for our little community," Lily said. "We're quite the collection of misfits."

"Gifted misfits."

"The best kind." She smiled, but it faded quickly. "And the dark figure he saw? Black or brown coat?"

"That describes half the people in this town in winter."

"Including Vernon Holt."

"Including Vernon Holt," I agreed.

The door to the deli opened, letting in a gust of cold air and Flo. She went straight to the counter, exchanging a few words with the young woman working the register, who handed over a paper bag. Flo was turning to leave when she spotted me and made a beeline for our table, her expression troubled.

"Alexis, honey. I was hoping I'd run into you." She glanced at Lily. "Do you mind if I sit for a minute?"

"Of course not." I gestured to the empty chair. "Is everything okay?"

Flo set her paper bag on the floor and sank into the seat, looking more frazzled than I'd ever seen her. "I need to talk to someone, and I don't know who else to trust. It's about that man who got killed. Grant."

Lily and I exchanged a glance. "What about him?"

Flo lowered her voice, leaning in. "I should have said something sooner. But with everything happening, and the diner being so busy, I just kept putting it off."

"Said something about what?"

"About Vernon Holt." She took a shaky breath. "He came into my diner about a week ago. Maybe ten days. And Grant was there, having breakfast like he did most mornings."

I leaned forward slightly. At game night, Gabe had mentioned Vernon complaining about Grant trespassing. But Flo had actually witnessed something.

"What happened?"

"Vernon came storming in, looking for Grant specifically. Said he'd seen him poking around on his property. Up near his cabin, where those old mining claims are." Flo shook her head. "Vernon's always been protective of that land. His grandfather worked those mines, you know. Before they dried up."

"What did he say to Grant?"

"Told him to stay away. That if he caught him up there again, there'd be trouble." Flo's voice dropped even lower. "He said, 'I've got a rifle and I know how to use it.' Those were his exact words."

A chill ran down my spine. "Did Grant respond?"

"Tried to play it off. Said he was just hiking, looking for good spots to photograph for his travel writing. But Vernon wasn't buying it. He got right up in Grant's face, close enough that I thought I might have to call Iris." She sighed. "Eventually Vernon left, but he was muttering the whole way out. Something about people always trying to take what wasn't theirs."

"Have you told Sheriff Iris about this?"

"That's the thing." Flo looked genuinely distressed, her eyes growing moist. She grabbed a napkin from the dispenser on the table and dabbed at them. "I meant to. But then Vernon came in yesterday, and he was so upset about the murder. Kept saying it was terrible, that nobody deserves to die like that. He seemed genuinely shaken." She met my eyes, still clutching the napkin. "Vernon's prickly and he's got a temper, but I've known him for thirty years. I can't imagine him actually killing someone."

"But you think the sheriff should know about the threat."

"I do. I'm going to tell her today, after I leave here." Flo twisted the napkin in her hands. "I just wanted to tell you first. You've got a way of figuring things out, Alexis. Better than most."

"I appreciate you trusting me with this."

"There's something else." Flo hesitated. "The morning Grant went up to the falls, he stopped by the diner early. Before six. I was just opening up."

"Did he seem different? Nervous?"

"He seemed excited. Almost giddy, which wasn't like him at all. Usually he was so tense, always looking over his shoulder." She frowned, remembering. "He ordered coffee to go and said something strange. 'Today's the day, Flo. Everything's finally coming together.' I asked him what he meant, but he just smiled and left."

Today's the day. Everything's finally coming together. What had Grant been planning? Had he been going to retrieve something? Meet someone?

"Thank you, Flo. This is really helpful."

"I hope so." She stood, gathering her coat and the paper bag she'd set on the floor. "I should get to the sheriff's station before I lose my nerve. You two take care of yourselves, you hear? There's something dark going on in this town."

She paused, her expression softening. "You know, you're both welcome at Sunday dinner anytime. The girls would love to see you. Ella's been asking about you, Alexis. Says you promised to teach her something."

A pang of guilt hit me. Ella, Flo's granddaughter, who could sense magic and hear animals speak. I'd been meaning to work with her more, help her understand her emerging gifts the way Maeve was helping Atticus. But with everything happening, I'd let it slip.

"I'd like that," I said. "Soon. I promise."

"Once things settle down," Flo said with a knowing smile. "In this town, that might be a while. But the invitation stands. Always."

After she left, Lily pushed her empty soup bowl aside. "So Vernon threatened Grant with a rifle. And Grant was excited about something the morning he died."

"The money, maybe. Whatever he stole and hid. Maybe he was finally going to retrieve it."

"Which means someone might have followed him. Someone who knew what he was after."

"Albert." The name tasted bitter in my mouth. "He's been asking about Grant's belongings. About his laptop."

"And then there's Martin Oakes," Lily added. "I assume you saw him outside the general store?"

"You saw him too?"

"Spotted him when I was walking here. He was watching the street, scanning everyone who passed." She frowned. "He's definitely looking for something. Or someone."

"Grant spent a lot of time in this town. At my café, at Flo's diner, walking the streets. If Martin Oakes is connected to Grant somehow, another victim maybe, or a PI hired by one of them..." I trailed off. "He might be hoping to find whatever Grant hid."

"So, we've got Albert Crane, who's definitely dangerous. And Martin Oakes, who's definitely watching. And we still don't know if they're connected," Lily said.

"Or if they're connected at all." I rubbed my temples. "Grant made a lot of enemies. Maybe they're all just circling, hoping to find whatever he hid."

"We need to crack that password. See what Grant was hiding."

I glanced at my phone. Two-thirty. "We have time before four. Want to walk around a bit? Clear our heads before we go to Maeve's?"

We paid for lunch and stepped out into the bright, cold afternoon. The sun was already beginning its descent toward the mountains, the shadows lengthening across the snow-covered streets. In an hour and a half, we'd be at Maeve's bookshop, attempting a spell that might unlock all of Grant's secrets.

Or might reveal dangers we weren't prepared for.

"Whatever's on that laptop," Lily said, as if reading my thoughts, "we'll face it together."

"Together," I agreed.

And we walked toward The Turning Page, toward answers, toward whatever came next.

# Chapter Nine

The Turning Page was quiet when we arrived, the closed sign hanging in the window. But the door was unlocked, and warm light spilled from the back room where Maeve kept her more esoteric supplies.

"Come in, come in," Maeve called as the bell chimed. "I've been expecting you."

We found her in the back, surrounded by candles and crystals and the laptop sitting open on a velvet cloth. The screen was dark, waiting for a password we didn't have. Yet.

"Before we begin," Maeve said, gesturing for us to sit, "there's something I want to discuss. Atticus Monroe."

I settled into one of the worn armchairs. "He came to see me this morning. He's struggling, but I think he's ready to accept what's happening to him."

"He is. I've been watching him for years, waiting for his gift to fully awaken." Maeve poured tea from a pot that seemed to stay perpetually warm. "Now that it has, he needs guidance. Proper training."

"What kind of training?" Lily asked.

"His gift is animal communion, similar to yours, Alexis, but broader. You hear cats specifically. Atticus can connect with any animal, though birds seem to be his strongest affinity." Maeve handed us each a cup. "Without training, he'll be overwhelmed. Every creature within range will flood his senses. He needs to learn to filter, to control when he opens himself and when he closes."

"How did you learn?" I asked. "To control your visions?"

"Slowly. Painfully. With a teacher who had more patience than I deserved." She smiled at the memory. "I'd like to spare Atticus some of that difficulty, if I can. But I'll need help."

"What can we do?"

"You can be his community. His support system." Maeve looked between us. "Learning to manage a gift is easier when you're not alone. When you have people who understand what you're going through. Lily, your gift with auras and emotional residue could help him understand how to read the feelings animals project. Alexis, your experience with cats could show him how to build relationships with specific creatures rather than being flooded by all of them."

"Like focusing on one voice in a crowded room," I said.

"Exactly. We'll start with simple exercises. Meditation. Grounding. Then gradually expose him to controlled connections." Maeve set down her teacup. "I was thinking we could meet weekly. Here, at the shop. A little coven of our own."

Lily laughed softly. "I like that. Though maybe don't call it a coven around Atticus just yet. He's still getting used to the idea that magic is real."

The word coven reminded me of something I'd been meaning to ask. "Maeve, there's something else. Something that happened last night."

"Oh?"

"I was at dinner in Silverpine with Colton. Twenty miles outside of town." I wrapped my hands around my teacup, drawing warmth from it. "And I felt something. That prickling sensation at the back of my neck, like being watched. Like something old and patient had its attention fixed on me."

Maeve's expression grew serious. "You're sure it wasn't just nerves? You've been under a great deal of stress."

"I'm sure. Lily felt it too, the night before. Here in town, we assumed it was the ley lines being attentive. But Silverpine isn't on the convergence."

"No, it isn't." Maeve was quiet for a long moment, her fingers tracing the rim of her teacup. "I've felt something too. A disturbance in the wards around town. Nothing broken, nothing breached. Just... pressure. As if something is testing the boundaries."

My stomach tightened. "The coven?"

"I don't know. It could be residual energy from the murder. Violent death leaves traces, especially near ley lines. It could be the convergence itself, reacting to the influx of strangers and tension." She met my eyes. "Or it could be something else entirely. Something that's been searching for a long time and is finally getting close."

"That's not reassuring."

"It's not meant to be. It's meant to be honest." Maeve reached across and squeezed my hand. "The wards are holding, Alexis. Whatever is watching, it hasn't found a way through. Not yet.

But we should be vigilant. If you feel that sensation again, tell me immediately."

"I will."

"For now, let's focus on what we can control. The laptop. The murder." She released my hand and turned toward the table. "One problem at a time."

"Fair point."

Maeve's eyes twinkled, though I could see the concern lingering beneath. "Now then. Shall we see what secrets Mr. Granger was hiding?"

She moved to the table where the laptop waited, and Lily and I followed. The candles flickered as we arranged ourselves around it, casting dancing shadows on the walls.

"This spell is different from what we did at the library," Maeve explained. "There, we were reading what the computer had displayed. Here, we're reading the keyboard itself. The keys Grant pressed most often, the emotions he felt when typing them."

"Will that really give us his password?" I asked.

"Passwords are interesting things. They're usually meaningful to the person who created them. Names, dates, significant words. Grant typed his password hundreds of times, each time with a particular emotional charge." She looked at Lily. "That repetition leaves traces. Echoes of intention. Your gift with auras and emotional residue makes you the best choice to read them."

"What do you need me to do?" Lily asked.

"Place your hands on the keyboard. Feel for the keys with the strongest emotional imprint. I'll ground the spell, keep it stable so you don't get overwhelmed." She glanced at me. "Alexis, you anchor Lily. Keep her tethered to the present so she doesn't get lost in Grant's emotions."

We took our positions. I stood behind Lily, my hands resting lightly on her shoulders. Maeve sat across the table, her palms flat against the wood, her eyes half-closed in concentration.

"Whenever you're ready," Maeve said.

Lily placed her hands on the keyboard, her fingers spread across the keys. For a moment, nothing happened. Then her breath caught.

"Fear," she whispered. "So much fear. He was terrified every time he touched this." Her brow furrowed. "But there's something else underneath. Determination. And... hope?"

"Focus on the keys," Maeve instructed gently. "Which ones carry the strongest charge?"

Lily's fingers moved slightly, hovering over different letters. "G. Strong anxiety here. And R. A. N. T." She frowned. "He typed his own name? Into his password?"

"Arrogance or carelessness," Maeve murmured. "Keep going."

More letters emerged as Lily traced the emotional residue. "H. I. K. E. R."

"Hiker," I said softly. "His cover story. The travel writer researching trails."

"There's more." Lily's voice had taken on a distant quality, her gift pulling her deeper into the impressions. "Numbers. Three. Zero. Zero."

"Three hundred," Maeve said. "Three hundred what?"

Lily gasped, her whole body tensing under my hands. I gripped her shoulders more firmly, keeping her grounded.

"Money," she breathed. "Three hundred thousand dollars. Guilt and triumph all tangled together. That's what he stole. That's what he was hiding."

"Lily," I said firmly. "Come back. That's enough."

She blinked, pulling her hands away from the keyboard. Her face was pale, a thin sheen of sweat on her forehead.

"Are you okay?" I asked.

"That was intense." She rubbed her temples. "Grant was a mess inside. Layers of fear and guilt and greed, all wrapped around each other."

"But we have enough," Maeve said. "The password. Let's try it."

My fingers were trembling slightly as I reached for the keyboard.

"GRANTHIKER300?" Lily suggested.

I typed it in. The screen flashed red. Incorrect password.

"Too simple," Maeve said. "Try combining them differently."

"HIKER300GRANT?"

Incorrect.

"Wait." Lily closed her eyes, thinking. "It wasn't his name first. It was the hope. The cover story. Then the guilt."

I typed: HIKERGRANT300

The screen flashed green. The desktop appeared.

"We're in," I whispered.

For a moment, we all just stared at the screen. A standard desktop background, a mountain landscape that could have been anywhere. A few folders. A handful of files.

"Let's see what he was hiding," Maeve said.

I clicked on the first folder, labeled "Research." Inside were dozens of documents. Trail guides. Hiking maps. Notes on local flora and fauna. Reviews of restaurants and hotels.

"His cover story," Lily said. "He really was writing travel content."

"Maintaining the illusion," Maeve agreed. "A good con artist always has a legitimate surface."

The next folder was labeled "Finances." When I opened it, my stomach dropped.

Spreadsheets. Dozens of them. Each one labeled with a different name. Dina Marsh. Opal Finch. Miriam Castellano. Winifred Baxter. More names I didn't recognize.

"His victims," I said quietly. The weight of it settled over me. Real people, real lives, reduced to entries in a spreadsheet.

Each spreadsheet contained detailed information. Amounts stolen. Dates. Methods. Notes on how he'd gained their trust, exploited their vulnerabilities, disappeared with their money.

"Forty thousand from Dina," Lily read over my shoulder. "Sixty-five thousand from Opal. Eighty thousand from Miriam." She shook her head. "He ruined their lives. Just numbers to him."

"Look at this one," I said, pointing to an entry for a woman named Opal Finch. Under "Notes," Grant had written: "Widow. Lonely. Desperate for connection. Easy."

"Easy," Lily repeated, her voice tight with anger. "He called her easy."

"He was a predator," Maeve said quietly. "Whatever else we learn about his death, we shouldn't forget that."

At the bottom of the list was a file with no name attached. Just a label: "The Big One."

I clicked on it.

The spreadsheet was different from the others. No personal details. No notes about emotional manipulation. Just a date, a location, and a transfer record.

"Denver," I read. "Eighteen months ago. Three hundred thousand dollars, wire transfer."

"Who did he steal it from?" Lily asked.

I scrolled down, looking for more information. But unlike the other files, this one was sparse. Almost deliberately vague. No name. No description of the mark. Just one cryptic note: "Not a person. An organization. Do NOT make contact."

"An organization," Maeve repeated slowly. "That's different from his usual targets."

"And dangerous," I added. "He was afraid of whoever he stole from. That's why there's no details."

"There's more." I pointed to another line. "'Package secured. Insurance in place. Retrieval contingent on safety.'"

"Package," Lily said. "He hid the money somewhere. Called it a package."

"And the insurance?"

I looked for more files. There was one labeled "Insurance," but when I clicked on it, a password prompt appeared.

"Another password," I muttered. "Of course."

I tried HIKERGRANT300 again. Incorrect.

"We'll have to crack this one separately," Maeve said. "But we have enough to work with. The victims. The amount. The reference to a hidden package."

"The morning he died," I said, remembering what Flo had told us, "Grant said 'Today's the day. Everything's finally coming together.' Maybe he was going to retrieve the money. The package."

"Which means he knew where it was hidden," Lily added. "And someone else might have known too. Someone who followed him to the falls."

"But who?" I stared at the screen. "If he stole from an organization, they could have sent anyone. Someone we've never even seen."

"Or someone hiding in plain sight," Maeve said grimly. "Pretending to be a grieving friend. Asking questions about belongings."

Albert. We were all thinking it. But we couldn't be sure. He could be working for the organization. He could be the organization. Or he could be exactly what he claimed to be, and the real killer was someone else entirely.

There was one more folder I hadn't opened. Labeled simply "Location."

I clicked on it.

Inside was a single document. A set of GPS coordinates. A photograph of a rocky outcropping near a waterfall. And a note:

"30 paces from bent pine. Due east. Behind loose rocks in split boulder."

"The falls," Lily breathed. "He hid the money near Aspen Falls."

"Where he died," I said. "He went to retrieve it, and someone killed him before he could." I paused, something clicking into place. "He'd been asking Atticus about hiding spots on the trails. But he already knew exactly where it was. He must have been trying to find a better location. Or making sure no one else knew about the one he'd already chosen."

We all stared at the screen, the implications settling over us like a cold weight.

"The killer might not have found it," Maeve said slowly. "If Grant was killed before he reached the hiding spot..."

"Then three hundred thousand dollars is still out there," I finished. "Hidden in the rocks near Aspen Falls."

"And whoever killed him is still searching for it."

Lily stood abruptly, pacing the small room. "We have to tell Iris. Show her what we found."

"We can't show her how we found it," I reminded her. "But we can tell her what we know. That Grant was running a long con. That he stole from dangerous people. That the money might still be hidden near the falls."

"What about the laptop?"

Maeve considered. "We could leave it somewhere it might be found. Let someone discover it and turn it in to the sheriff."

"That feels dishonest."

"It protects you. Both of you." Maeve's voice was gentle but firm. "You've done nothing wrong except try to solve a murder. But if Iris asks how you cracked a password-protected laptop, what will you tell her?"

I didn't have an answer for that.

"For now," Maeve said, "we keep the laptop here. Hidden and warded. We tell Iris what we've learned through other means. The gossip at game night. Flo's account of the confrontation with Vernon. The information Dina shared about Grant being a con artist."

"And if she asks how we know about the money?"

"Dina mentioned rumors. That Grant had gotten in over his head, stolen from someone dangerous." Maeve began snuffing the candles, the spell work complete. "You're simply following those rumors to their logical conclusion."

It wasn't perfect. But it was something.

"What about our suspects?" Lily asked. "Vernon threatened Grant with a rifle. Albert's been asking questions about Grant's things. And there's Martin Oakes, the man who's been watching the café and the town. The one Flo mentioned from her diner."

"The one with the forgettable face," I added. "He's been surveilling all the places Grant frequented. Like he's looking for something."

"Or someone," Maeve said thoughtfully. "He could be working for one of Grant's victims. A private investigator, perhaps, hired to track down the stolen money."

"And Dina," I added reluctantly. "She says she wanted her money back, that dead men can't write checks. But she also admitted to fantasizing about killing him for months."

"A woman scorned," Maeve said. "Never underestimate that particular fury."

"Any of them could be connected to the organization Grant stole from," I said. "Or working alone for their own reasons. We need more information before we can narrow it down."

The sun had fully set by the time we left The Turning Page. The streets were quiet, most of Larkspur Valley tucked inside for Sunday dinner. I thought about Flo's invitation, her warm kitchen, her crowded table full of love and chaos.

Soon, I promised myself. Once this was over. Once we'd found out who killed Grant and why.

But for now, there was work to do.

"Tomorrow," I said as Lily and I walked home through the cold night air, "we need to learn more about our suspects. All of them. Albert, Vernon, Dina, and Martin Oakes."

"And Iris?"

"Her too. Carefully. Strategically."

Lily linked her arm through mine. "You know, for someone who just wanted a quiet life running a cat café, you're remarkably good at solving murders."

I laughed despite myself. "Maybe that's my real gift. Not talking to cats. Just stumbling into trouble."

"Some gift."

"Tell me about it."

Above us, stars were beginning to appear through breaks in the clouds. Somewhere in the darkness, a killer was still free. Somewhere, three hundred thousand dollars was hidden in the rocks near a frozen waterfall.

And somewhere, something old and patient was watching. Testing the wards. Getting closer.

But we had answers now. Pieces of the puzzle that hadn't existed before.

Tomorrow, we'd start putting them together.

# Chapter Ten

Monday morning started like any other. I was downstairs before dawn, prepping the café, grinding beans, arranging pastries from Flo's latest delivery. The cats took their positions around the room, Poppy on her heated bed, Gus on his high perch, Rocky prowling for crumbs, Millie tucked behind her fern, and Sage curled in a patch of early sunlight.

"You slept better last night," Poppy observed. "Fewer dreams."

"We found some answers yesterday. It helps."

"But not all the answers."

"No. Not yet."

My phone buzzed with a text from Colton: "Hope you had a good Sunday. Thinking about you. Dinner this weekend?"

I typed back: "Sunday was busy but good. Dinner sounds nice. I'll let you know my schedule."

Three dots appeared, then: "Can't wait. Talk soon."

It was sweet. Attentive. The kind of thing that should make me smile. And it did, mostly. But there was something about the steady certainty of his texts that made me feel like I was being slowly collected. Like he'd already decided how this would go, and I was just catching up.

I shook off the thought. Colton was a good man. I was lucky he was interested.

Lily arrived at seven, looking more energized than she had in days. "I've been thinking about what we found on the laptop," she said as she tied on her apron. "The location file. The coordinates near the falls."

"What about it?"

"If Grant was killed before he could retrieve the money, it's still there. Hidden in those rocks." She lowered her voice. "Should we go look for it?"

I'd been thinking the same thing. Three hundred thousand dollars, sitting in a crevice near Aspen Falls. Evidence that could help solve the murder. Or a target that could get us killed.

"Not yet," I said. "We need to be careful. If the killer is still looking for it..."

"They might be watching the falls. Waiting to see if anyone goes poking around."

"Exactly."

The door chimed, and Cordelia bustled in, her yarn bag over one shoulder and her eyes bright with the particular gleam that meant she had news to share.

"Did you hear?" she asked before she'd even reached the counter. "About Grant Granger's cabin?"

I felt Lily tense beside me. "What about it?"

"Ransacked!" Cordelia practically vibrated with the thrill of being first with the news. "Someone broke in and tore the place apart. Mabel heard it from her nephew, who works at the lodge. The maid went to clean the cabin yesterday evening and found it completely destroyed."

"Destroyed how?"

"Furniture overturned, drawers emptied, mattress slashed open." Cordelia leaned in conspiratorially. "They were looking for something. Something Grant had hidden."

My mind raced. The laptop was safe at Maeve's. But whoever had ransacked the cabin didn't know that. They were still searching.

"Does Sheriff Iris know?" I asked.

"Oh, she knows. She's been up there since last night, apparently." Cordelia accepted the lavender tea I'd started making automatically. "But that's not even the most interesting part."

"There's more?"

"Vernon Holt was caught near the cabin. You know, that rental place just down the trail from his property. He said he heard sounds and went to investigate, but Iris isn't buying it." She shook her head. "I always said there was something off about that man. Living up in the hills all alone, threatening people with rifles. It was only a matter of time before he snapped."

"Has he been arrested?"

"Detained, is what I heard. For further questioning." Cordelia took her tea and settled into her usual spot by the window. "Mark my words, he's the one who did it. Killed that poor man and then went back to search for whatever Grant was hiding."

After she'd settled in, more customers trickled in, each one bringing their own version of the news. The details shifted with each telling, growing more elaborate and dramatic. By nine o'clock, I'd heard that Vernon had been found standing over the ransacked cabin with blood on his hands, that he'd confessed to everything, that he'd been caught trying to flee town.

None of it matched what Cordelia had originally said, which made me suspect none of it was true.

"Small town telephone," Lily muttered during a brief lull. "The story changes every time someone tells it."

"The question is what actually happened." I glanced at the clock. Nine-thirty. Iris usually came in for her coffee by eight. "And where's Iris? She's never this late."

"Busy, probably. If she's been at the cabin since last night..."

The door chimed, and I looked up hoping to see Iris. Instead, it was Lionel.

He was dressed casually, no comic book characters on his shirt today, just a simple blue sweater that made his eyes look even warmer than usual. He smiled when he saw me, that quiet smile that never demanded anything.

"Morning," he said, approaching the counter. "I heard about the break-in at Grant's cabin. Wanted to make sure you were okay."

"I'm fine. A little rattled by all the gossip, but fine."

"It's all anyone's talking about at the shop. I've had three customers come in just to speculate about whether Vernon did it." He shook his head. "I keep telling them to let Iris do her job, but you know how people are."

"I do."

He ordered his usual dandelion root tea, and I made it while he waited. Unlike Colton, who always seemed to fill silence with plans and observations, Lionel was comfortable just being quiet. Standing at the counter, watching me work, not needing to fill every moment with words.

"How was your weekend?" he asked as I handed him the cup. "Besides, you know, all this?"

"It was..." I thought about the date with Colton. The spell at Maeve's. The feeling of being watched in Silverpine. "Complicated."

"Complicated good or complicated bad?"

"Complicated complicated."

He laughed softly. "Fair enough. If you ever want to talk about it, you know where to find me." He raised his cup in a small salute. "Take care of yourself, Alexis."

"You too."

He left without lingering, without asking when he'd see me again, without making any claims on my time or attention. Just a simple check-in, a moment of warmth, and then gone.

"He's a good one," Lily said quietly after the door closed behind him.

"I know."

"So is Colton."

"I know that too."

"Quite the dilemma."

I didn't have an answer for that, so I just kept wiping down the counter.

The door chimed again, and this time it was Esther James, looking harried and juggling her wallet.

"Please tell me you have a fresh pot going," she said as she reached the counter. "I'm on my planning period and I promised half the English department I'd make a coffee run. Everyone's too distracted to function."

"That bad?"

"My students spent first period whispering about the break-in instead of discussing symbolism in The Great Gatsby." She pulled out a scrap of paper with scribbled orders. "Let's see. Two black coffees, one with cream, one Earl Grey, and whatever's strongest for me."

"We've been hearing about it all morning," I said as I started making her drinks. "Do you know what actually happened?"

"Only what Gabe told me. He ran into one of the deputies at the hardware store earlier." She accepted the first coffee gratefully, taking a sip before I could tell her it was one of the black ones for her colleagues. "Apparently Vernon claims he was walking past the cabin on his way down from his property when he heard sounds. Crashing, like someone throwing things around. He says he went to investigate and found the place already torn apart. Called out, but whoever did it was already gone."

"And Iris doesn't believe him?"

"Would you? Vernon's been vocal about his dislike of Grant. Threatened him publicly. And now he just happens to be at the scene of a break-in?" Esther shook her head. "It doesn't look good for him."

"What about an alibi? For the night of the murder?"

"That's the problem. Vernon lives alone. No one to vouch for his whereabouts." I handed her a cardboard carrier with the rest of the drinks, and she balanced it carefully. "I need to get back before the bell. But be careful, Alexis. If Vernon isn't the killer, then whoever is, is still out there. Still looking for whatever Grant was hiding."

After she left, the café settled into a quieter rhythm. The morning rush had passed, leaving only a handful of customers nursing their drinks and murmuring to each other about the latest developments.

Through the window, I caught sight of a familiar figure across the street. Martin Oakes, standing outside the hardware store, apparently examining the window display. But his attention wasn't on the tools and supplies. He was watching the street again, that patient, professional surveillance I'd come to recognize.

Still looking for something. Or someone.

I was wiping down the counter when the door opened and Iris finally walked in.

She looked exhausted, dark circles under her eyes even more pronounced than before. Her uniform was rumpled, her hair escaping from its usual neat braid. She moved like someone running on coffee and determination alone.

"The usual?" I asked.

"Please. To go." She leaned against the counter, and for a moment, the professional mask slipped. She just looked tired. "It's been a long night."

"I heard about the cabin. And Vernon."

"News travels fast." She accepted the coffee I handed her, wrapping both hands around the cup. "Vernon's story is... not impossible. But it's convenient. Too convenient."

"You think he did it? Killed Grant and then went back to search the cabin?"

"I think he had motive, opportunity, and was found at the scene of a crime." She took a long sip of coffee. "But thinking isn't proving. We're still working on that."

"What about the others? The woman from Denver, Dina Marsh?"

Iris's expression flickered. "She's being questioned too. Her alibi for the night of the murder has some holes in it. She claims she was at the lodge all evening, but no one can confirm she didn't leave."

"And the man who came in asking about Grant? Albert Crane?"

"Him too. Everyone who had contact with Grant is being looked at." She straightened, the professional mask sliding back into place. "I shouldn't be telling you any of this."

"I'm just worried. About the town. About whoever's doing this."

"I know." Her voice softened slightly. "You've been helpful before, Alexis. With the other cases. But this one..." She shook her head. "This one feels different. Bigger. Like there's something underneath that I'm not seeing."

"If I hear anything that might help..."

"You'll tell me. I know." She managed a tired smile. "Thanks for the coffee. I'll be back when I can."

After she left, Lily joined me at the counter.

"So, Vernon's detained, Dina's being questioned, and Albert's on the radar," she said quietly. "But no one's been arrested."

"Which means Iris doesn't have enough evidence to charge anyone."

"Or she's not sure which one actually did it."

I thought about what Iris had said. That this case felt bigger. That there was something underneath she wasn't seeing.

She was right. There was something underneath. Three hundred thousand dollars hidden near a waterfall. An organization that Grant had been afraid to even name. Secrets locked behind a password we hadn't cracked yet.

"We need to find out more," I said. "About all of them. Vernon, Dina, Albert. And whoever else Grant might have crossed."

"How?"

Before I could answer, the door chimed again. This time it was Martin Oakes.

I recognized him immediately, despite those forgettable features. Medium build, brown hair going gray, the kind of face your eyes would slide right past if you weren't paying attention. But I was paying attention now. And so were the cats.

Rocky, who had been cleaning himself, stopped mid lick, one back leg held straight up in the air, and let out a low growl. It was completely undignified, yet somehow menacing. I had to stop myself from laughing.

"Hush," I murmured.

Martin approached the counter with quick, slightly jerky movements. Up close, I could see the tension in his shoulders, the way his eyes kept darting to the door and windows. For all his professional surveillance manner, he was nervous about something today.

"Coffee," he said. "Black. To go."

His voice was clipped, impatient. Nothing like the patient watcher I'd observed from a distance.

"Coming right up," I said, keeping my voice neutral. "You've been in before, haven't you?"

He flinched slightly at the question. "Once. Maybe twice. I'm just passing through."

But he wasn't just passing through. I'd seen him watching the café, watching Flo's diner, watching the street. He was here for a reason. And it had something to do with Grant.

"Anxious man," Rocky said from his shelf. "Smells like worry and searching. He's looking for something he hasn't found."

Gus appeared at the end of the counter, watching Martin with unblinking eyes. "Not dangerous like the cold one. But not safe either."

"That's four fifty," I said, handing Martin the cup.

He paid in cash, exact change, and left without another word. Through the window, I watched him hurry down Main Street, glancing over his shoulder once before disappearing around a corner. Less patient today. More rattled.

"That's the man who's been watching the town," Lily said softly. "Martin Oakes."

"I know. And I remember now. He came in once before. The day Grant died, right after Grant left for the falls the second time. A forgettable face, medium build, brown hair going gray. He stepped inside, scanned the room, and left without ordering anything. At the time I thought it was odd but didn't think more of it. Now I think he was looking for Grant."

"Someone from Grant's past?"

"Must be. Another victim, maybe. Or a PI hired by one of them to track down the money." I thought about Maeve's suggestion from last night. "He's been watching all the places Grant frequented. Waiting for something to surface."

"The laptop. The money."

"Probably. And now that Grant's cabin has been ransacked, he knows someone else is looking too." I wiped down the counter, thinking. "We should tell Iris about him. About the connection to Grant."

"If she doesn't already know."

"If she doesn't already know."

The door chimed again, and I tensed. But it was just Mabel Smalls, come for her usual morning crossword and chamomile tea. She settled into her favorite booth by the window, puzzle book already open before I'd even brought her drink.

Normal. Familiar. Safe.

But nothing in Larkspur Valley felt safe anymore.

The rest of the late morning passed quietly. Too quietly, after the chaos of the early hours. I kept thinking about Vernon, detained at the sheriff's station. About Dina, with her holes in her alibi. About Albert Crane, with his cold eyes and careful questions. And about Martin Oakes, watching and waiting, connected to Grant in ways we didn't yet understand.

One of them had killed Grant. One of them had ransacked his cabin, searching for whatever he'd hidden.

And one of them might come after us next, if they figured out we had his laptop.

"We need to be careful," I said to Lily as the lunch crowd started to trickle in. "Really careful."

"I know."

"And we need to find out what's in that insurance file. The one we couldn't crack."

"Maeve might have ideas."

"Then we talk to Maeve. Tonight, after closing."

Lily nodded, her expression determined. "Tonight."

I glanced over at Mabel, still happily working her crossword, oblivious to the danger swirling around our little town. I envied her that peace. That certainty that the world was still orderly, still safe. But I knew better now. And I couldn't unknow it.

## Chapter Eleven

The afternoon crowd was lighter than usual, people apparently more interested in gossiping at home than venturing out for coffee. I didn't mind. After the chaos of the morning, the quiet felt like a gift.

Mabel had long since finished her crossword and departed with a cheerful wave. The lunch rush had come and gone, leaving behind a few scattered cups and empty pastry plates. Lily and I worked in comfortable silence, restocking supplies and wiping down tables, both of us counting the hours until closing.

"Do you think you'll be able to crack the insurance file tonight?" I asked as Lily refilled the sugar dispensers.

"With Maeve's help, I think so. The first password worked because of emotional residue. This one might be trickier, but I can try." She glanced at the clock. "Four-thirty. An hour and a half until we can close."

"The question is what we'll find when we do."

"Evidence, hopefully. Something that points to who killed Grant."

"Or something that makes us an even bigger target than we already are."

The cats had been unusually subdued all day, picking up on the tension that seemed to permeate everything. Poppy watched the door from her heated bed, her eyes tracking every customer who entered. Gus had barely moved from his high perch, a silent sentinel. Even Rocky had abandoned his usual chaos, content to doze in a patch of fading sunlight.

Only Sage seemed unbothered, chasing dust motes near the window with her typical kitten enthusiasm.

"To be young and oblivious," Lily said, watching her.

"She's not oblivious. She just hasn't learned to be afraid yet."

Poppy stretched and jumped down from her bed, padding over to where I stood behind the counter. "We should be helping," she said. "Investigating. Finding the person who did this."

"You are helping. You're keeping watch."

"From inside." Her tail flicked with frustration. "We could do more if you let us go outside. Follow scents. Listen to conversations. Cats hear things humans miss."

Rocky lifted his head, suddenly interested. "Yes! Outside! I could track the cold man. Find where he's staying. Sniff out his secrets."

"Absolutely not."

"But we're good at investigating," Rocky protested. "Remember the poison case? I found the—"

"You found a clue inside the café," I said firmly. "Outside is different. Outside is dangerous."

Gus descended from his perch with unusual speed, joining the conversation. "She's right. The outside has teeth."

"Teeth?" Sage had abandoned her dust motes, drawn by the discussion. "What kind of teeth?"

"Wolves," I said. "Coyotes. Mountain lions. They all live in these mountains, and they all think cats look like dinner." I crouched down to their level, meeting Poppy's steady gaze. "Not to mention cars. Stray dogs. Hawks that would love to snatch up a small cat."

"I'm not small," Rocky said indignantly.

"You're small enough." I scratched behind his ears. "I know you want to help. But I can't risk losing any of you. Not for a murder investigation. Not for anything."

Poppy was quiet for a moment, then sighed. "We understand. But it's frustrating. Sitting inside while danger circles."

"I know. Believe me, I know."

Millie emerged from behind her fern, her blue eyes wide. "The cold man is very bad," she said softly. "I can feel it when he comes in. Like ice in my fur. Promise you'll be careful too?"

"I promise."

The door chimed, and we all looked up. Martin Oakes stepped inside, moving with that same quick, slightly nervous energy I'd noticed earlier. He glanced around the café, taking in the nearly empty room, before approaching the counter.

"Coffee," he said. "Black. To go. Please."

I made his drink while he stood fidgeting near the register, his eyes darting to the window every few seconds.

"Busy day?" I asked, keeping my tone casual.

He gave a short, humorless laugh. "You could say that." He shook his head. "I thought this was supposed to be a quiet mountain town. Peaceful. Instead, there's a murder, a break-in, people getting detained..." He trailed off, seeming to catch himself. "Not exactly what I expected when I arrived."

"When did you arrive?" I asked, handing him the cup.

Something flickered in his expression. Wariness, maybe. "A week or so ago. Just passing through, originally. But things got... complicated."

"Complicated how?"

He studied me for a moment, and I had the sense he was deciding how much to say. "Let's just say I'm looking for something. Someone owed me answers, and this is where the trail led." He pulled out exact change and set it on the counter. "Thanks for the coffee."

He was out the door before I could respond, hurrying down Main Street with his collar turned up against the cold.

"Looking for something," Lily said quietly. "Or someone."

"He's connected to Grant somehow. I'm more sure of it every time I see him." I watched him disappear around a corner. "But I don't think he's the killer. He's too... anxious. Too unsettled. Albert Crane is controlled. Calculated. This man is searching, not hunting."

"A victim, maybe? One of the people Grant conned?"

"Or a PI hired by one of them. Either way, he's not telling us everything."

My phone buzzed with a text from Colton: "Thinking about you. Hope your day is going okay. Let me know if you need anything."

I typed back a quick response: "Busy but okay. Talk later?"

His reply came almost immediately: "Always. I'm here whenever you need me."

It should have been comforting. It was comforting, in a way. But there was something about the constant availability, the steady certainty, that felt less like support and more like... waiting. Like he was always there, ready to step in, whether I needed him to or not.

I pushed the thought aside. Colton was being kind. That was all.

The door chimed at five o'clock, and I looked up expecting another local stopping in for an afternoon pick-me-up.

Instead, it was Albert Crane.

He moved through the café with that same controlled grace I'd noticed before, his eyes sweeping the room and cataloging everything. When his gaze landed on me, he smiled. It was a pleasant smile. A friendly smile. A smile that never quite reached his eyes.

"Good afternoon," he said as he approached the counter. "I was hoping I'd find you here."

Rocky lifted his head from his nap, a low growl rumbling in his throat. Gus went completely still on his perch. Even Millie, usually so timid, emerged slightly from behind her fern to watch the newcomer with wary eyes.

I reached down and scratched behind Rocky's ears, a subtle signal to stay calm.

"Can I get you something?" I asked, keeping my voice light and professional.

"Just a coffee. Black." He leaned against the counter, casual and unhurried. "I've been meaning to come back. Ask a few more questions about Grant, if you don't mind."

"I'm not sure how much help I can be. I already told you everything I know."

"Did you?" His tone was mild, but there was something sharp underneath. "I've been talking to people around town. Gathering information. And your name keeps coming up."

"I run a coffee shop. Everyone's name comes up eventually."

He smiled at that, acknowledging the point. "Fair enough. But people say Grant spent a lot of time here. More than just grabbing coffee. They say he sat for hours, working on his laptop."

Behind me, I felt Lily tense. I kept my expression neutral.

"He did. Came in most mornings, ordered his usual, sat by the window and typed away." I shrugged. "Lots of people work here. We have good wifi."

"Did he ever talk to you? About what he was working on?"

"Not really. He said he was a travel writer, researching trails in the area. That's about it." I made his coffee, taking my time, using the routine to keep my hands steady. I put it in a to-go cup even though he hadn't asked for one. A subtle hint. "He wasn't much for conversation. Kept to himself mostly."

"And after he finished working? Did you notice where he went? What he did?"

"No idea. He'd pack up his things and head out. Whatever he did after that was his own business." I handed him the cup, meeting his eyes with practiced indifference. "Whatever that was."

Albert studied me for a long moment. I couldn't tell if he believed me or not. His face gave nothing away.

"You're very calm," he said finally. "For someone whose regular customer was just murdered."

"It's not my first time dealing with tragedy in this town. You learn to keep going."

"So I've heard." He took a sip of his coffee, still watching me over the rim. "The sheriff seems to think Vernon Holt might be responsible. What do you think?"

"I think that's for the sheriff to figure out, not me."

"But you have opinions. Everyone does."

I pretended to consider the question. "Vernon's got a temper, that's no secret. But I don't know him well enough to say whether he'd actually hurt someone. People surprise you, I guess. For better or worse."

Albert nodded slowly. "They certainly do."

He glanced around the café again, his gaze lingering on the back-room door. "Grant never left anything here, did he? A bag, maybe? Or his laptop?"

The question was casual. Too casual.

"No," I said. "He always took everything with him when he left."

"You're sure?"

"Positive. I would have noticed."

Another long look. Another moment of assessment. I could feel him weighing my words, searching for cracks in my composure.

"You know," he said slowly, "I'm just trying to find out what happened to my friend. Grant and I go back twenty years. His family deserves answers. Closure." His voice softened, but the effect felt rehearsed. "And if there are any of his personal effects out there, his belongings, I'd like to make sure they get back to the people who loved him."

The words sounded right. Caring. Reasonable. But they didn't match the coldness in his eyes.

"That's very thoughtful of you," I said carefully.

"It's what friends do." He picked up his cup again. "I've also noticed something interesting about this town. People here are very... loyal. Protective of each other. It's admirable, in a way." He took a sip. "But it can also be dangerous. Protecting the wrong person. Keeping the wrong secrets."

"I'm not sure what you mean."

"I think you do." His smile didn't waver, but his eyes had gone cold. "Grant made a lot of enemies, Alexis. Powerful enemies. The kind of people who don't give up easily. If someone in this town is hiding something that belongs to them..." He let the sentence hang. "Well. It wouldn't end well for that person."

The threat was unmistakable. My heart was pounding, but I kept my voice steady.

"Like I said, I don't know anything about Grant's belongings. But if you're concerned about dangerous people, you should probably talk to Sheriff Iris. That's her job."

"I've talked to her. She's very... thorough." He pulled out his wallet and left a twenty on the counter. "Keep the change."

"That's too much."

"Consider it a thank you. For your time." He tucked his wallet away, his movements precise and economical. "I'm sure I'll see you around, Alexis. It's a small town."

"It is."

He headed for the door, then paused, looking back at me. "One more thing. If you do happen to remember anything else about Grant, anything at all, I'd appreciate it if you'd let me know. I'm staying at the Pine Lodge. Room twelve."

"I'll keep that in mind."

The bell chimed as he left, and I watched him walk down Main Street until he disappeared around a corner. Only then did I let out the breath I'd been holding.

"That was terrifying," Lily said softly, appearing at my elbow.

"I know."

"He knows something. Or suspects something."

"I know."

"And that threat about powerful enemies..."

"I know."

Rocky jumped onto the counter, pressing his head against my hand. "Bad man," he said. "Very dangerous. He meant what he said about things not ending well."

"I believe you, Rocky." I stroked his fur, trying to calm my racing heart. "I believe you."

The last hour before closing crawled by. A few more customers trickled in and out, but I barely registered them. My mind kept replaying the conversation with Albert. The questions he'd asked. The way he'd looked at the back-room door. The thinly veiled threat about powerful enemies.

He was hunting for the laptop. He had to be. And if he found out we had it...

At six o'clock, I flipped the sign to Closed with more relief than I'd ever felt. Lily and I cleaned up in record time, neither of us speaking, both of us eager to get to Maeve's.

"Should we be worried?" Lily asked as we bundled into our coats. "About Albert, I mean. About him coming after us."

"Probably. But worrying won't help." I locked the back door behind us, double-checking the bolt. "What will help is figuring out what Grant was hiding. The sooner we crack that insurance file, the sooner we can give Iris something concrete."

"And then?"

"And then we let her handle it. That's her job, not ours."

But even as I said it, I wasn't sure I believed it. Albert wasn't going to stop looking just because we handed information to the sheriff. He was too determined. Too dangerous.

The walk to The Turning Page was quiet, the streets empty in the early evening darkness. Christmas lights twinkled in shop windows, a cheerful contrast to the tension knotting my stomach.

"He asked about the laptop specifically," Lily said as we walked. "That can't be a coincidence."

"It's not. He knows Grant had one. He knows it's missing. And he's trying to figure out who has it."

"Do you think he suspects us?"

I thought about the way Albert had looked at me. The careful questions. The assessment in his eyes. The threat delivered with a smile, wrapped in that nonsense about closure for Grant's family.

"I think he suspects everyone. We're just one possibility among many." I stepped around a patch of ice on the sidewalk. "But that won't last forever. Sooner or later, he's going to narrow it down."

"Then we'd better figure this out fast."

"Yes. We'd better."

We were halfway there when I felt it.

That prickle at the back of my neck. That sense of being watched by something that had nothing to do with Albert Crane or Martin Oakes or murder investigations.

I stopped walking, scanning the street. Empty. Silent. Just snow and shadows and the distant glow of streetlights.

"What is it?" Lily asked.

"Do you feel that?"

She was quiet for a moment, her breath misting in the cold air. "Yes," she said finally. "Faint, but there. Like something brushing against the edge of my awareness."

"It's the same thing I felt in Silverpine. The same thing we felt near Maeve's." I wrapped my arms around myself, suddenly cold in a way that had nothing to do with the temperature. "It's getting stronger."

"Or closer."

Neither of us said anything else. We just walked faster, our footsteps crunching in the snow, until the warm lights of The Turning Page came into view.

I paused outside the shop, the glow from Maeve's windows spilling onto the snowy sidewalk. The feeling of being watched had faded, replaced by the familiar comfort of approaching a safe place.

"Whatever that was," Lily said quietly, "it's not following us here. Maeve's wards must be keeping it out."

"For now." I took a breath, steadying myself. "One problem at a time. Let's focus on what we can actually solve tonight."

I pushed open the door, the familiar chime announcing our arrival. Somewhere inside, Maeve was waiting with a laptop full of secrets and a password we hadn't cracked.

It was time to find out what Grant's insurance really was.

And hope it was enough to stop a killer.

# Chapter Twelve

The Turning Page was warm and glowing when we stepped inside, lamplight spilling across the worn wooden floors. The familiar scent of old books and dried herbs wrapped around me like a blanket, and some of the tension in my shoulders began to ease.

Then I heard voices from the back room, and the tension returned in full force.

I grabbed Lily's arm, pulling her to a stop. We exchanged a look, both of us thinking the same thing. Albert. He'd followed us. He'd found where Maeve kept the laptop.

We moved quietly toward the sound, footsteps soft on the creaking floor. My heart was pounding so loudly I was sure whoever was back there could hear it.

"...and the hawk came back this morning," a male voice was saying. "Landed on my windowsill like it was waiting for me. When I reached out, I could feel everything. The cold air, the mice moving under the snow, even the heartbeat of a rabbit hiding in the brush."

I let out a breath I hadn't realized I'd been holding. Atticus.

Maeve's voice responded, low and warm. "That's wonderful progress, Atticus. You're learning to connect without being overwhelmed."

Lily squeezed my hand, and we rounded the corner into the back room. Atticus sat across from Maeve, a cup of tea cradled in his hands. They both looked up at our entrance.

"Oh, good," Maeve said with a smile. "Y'all are here too."

"We didn't mean to interrupt," I said, still trying to slow my racing heart. "We heard voices and thought..."

"That it might be someone dangerous?" Maeve's eyes crinkled with understanding. "I should have warned you Atticus would be here. We were just finishing up his first official lesson."

"Perfect timing, actually," she added, gesturing for us to sit.

Lily and I settled into chairs across from Atticus.

"We have some work to do tonight," Maeve said carefully. "Something that might be educational for you to observe. If you're comfortable with that."

"What kind of work?"

I glanced at Lily, then at Maeve. She gave a small nod.

"We have Grant Granger's laptop," I said. "The man who was murdered. He left it at my café the day he died and never came back for it. There's a file on it we haven't been able to open. Lily's going to try to crack the password using her gift."

Atticus's eyes widened. "Her gift?"

"I can read emotional residue," Lily explained. "The feelings people leave behind on objects they've touched. It's similar to what you're developing with animals but focused on human emotions instead."

"And you can use that to figure out a password?"

"We've done something similar before. Last month, we used a spell to read what someone had been searching for on a library computer. The keys they pressed, the emotions behind their searches." She smiled slightly. "Passwords are even more personal. More meaningful. When someone types the same word hundreds of times, they leave strong traces of what that word means to them."

Atticus sat back, processing this. "And you want me to watch?"

"This will be a good thing for you to observe," Maeve said. "Understanding how others use their gifts can help you understand your own. The principles are similar, even if the applications are different. And when we work together, combining our abilities, we can accomplish things none of us could manage alone."

"Okay." He nodded slowly. "I'd like that."

Maeve rose and moved to a cabinet in the corner, pulling out the laptop wrapped in its protective velvet cloth. She set it on the table between us, and I felt the atmosphere in the room shift. Heavier. More charged.

"The file is called 'Insurance,'" I explained to Atticus as Maeve arranged candles around the workspace. "We think it contains information about who Grant stole from. Something he was using as leverage, maybe. Protection."

"Insurance against what?"

"Against the people who wanted him dead."

The candles flickered to life as Maeve lit them one by one. The laptop sat open on the table, the password prompt glowing on the screen.

"Same positions as before," Maeve said. "Lily, you read. Alexis, you anchor. I'll ground." She looked at Atticus. "You observe. Don't try to reach out or connect with anything. Just watch. Feel. Learn."

He nodded, his expression serious.

I moved behind Lily, placing my hands on her shoulders. Maeve sat across the table, her palms flat against the wood. Atticus remained in his chair, slightly back from the circle, his eyes wide and attentive.

"Whenever you're ready," Maeve said.

Lily placed her hands on the keyboard and closed her eyes.

For a long moment, nothing happened. The candles flickered. The room was silent except for our breathing. I could feel the tension in Lily's shoulders, the way she was reaching, stretching her gift toward the laptop.

Then her brow furrowed, and I felt her shoulders tense beneath my hands.

"This one's different," she murmured. "Harder to read. Like he was trying to hide even from himself."

"Take your time," Maeve said softly.

Lily pressed deeper. I could feel her reaching, stretching her gift beyond its usual limits. Sweat beaded on her forehead. Her breathing grew shallow.

From the corner of my eye, I saw Atticus lean forward in his chair, his face pale with concentration. He was feeling something too, picking up on the edges of the spell even without trying.

"Fear again. But older. Deeper." Lily's voice had taken on that distant quality I'd heard before. "This password isn't about hope or arrogance. It's about survival."

"What do you feel?" Maeve prompted.

"Numbers. A date, maybe. Something that happened to him." Her fingers twitched over the keys. "One. Nine. Eight. Seven."

"1987," I said. "The year he was born?"

"No. Something that happened in 1987. Something that changed him." Lily's breathing grew ragged. "There's a word attached. A place. Or a name. It's wrapped in so much pain..."

"Can you see it?"

"R. I. V..." She gasped, her whole body shuddering. "River. Blackriver. That's it. Blackriver1987."

"Lily," I said firmly, gripping her shoulders. "Come back now."

She pulled her hands away from the keyboard, slumping back against me. Her face was pale, her breathing uneven.

"Are you okay?" I asked.

"That was harder than the first one. He buried that password deep." She managed a weak smile. "But I got it."

I looked at Atticus. He was staring at Lily with something like awe, his face pale, his hands gripping the arms of his chair.

"That was..." He shook his head, apparently unable to find the words. "I could feel it. Not clearly, not the way she did, but there was something. A kind of pressure in the room. Like the air got heavier."

"You sensed the spell," Maeve said, looking pleased. "That's remarkable for someone so new to their gift."

"Is it always like that? That intense?"

"Sometimes more. Sometimes less." Maeve began snuffing the candles. "Magic has a cost. The deeper you reach, the more it takes from you."

"Blackriver," I said, turning the word over in my mind. "Does that mean anything to anyone?"

"Could be a town," Lily suggested, still recovering. "Or a river. There are probably dozens of places called Blackriver across the country."

"Whatever it is, something happened there in 1987 that marked Grant deeply enough to become his most secret password." Maeve looked thoughtful. "Something traumatic, by the feel of it. The kind of thing that shapes a person."

"Grant would have been... what, in his late forties?" I calculated. "So in 1987, he was maybe eight or nine years old."

"A childhood trauma," Lily said quietly. "Something that happened when he was just a boy."

For a moment, I almost felt sorry for Grant. Whatever had happened at Blackriver had left scars deep enough that he carried them into adulthood, turned them into the key to his darkest secrets.

"We'll never know what it was," I said. "Not now. Whatever story that password tells, Grant took it to his grave."

"Some mysteries stay mysteries," Maeve agreed.

Then I remembered Dina's face, remembered the spreadsheet full of victims, and the sympathy faded. Whatever had happened to Grant as a child didn't excuse what he'd done to others as a man.

"Let's see if it worked," Lily said, sitting up straighter.

I typed in the password: Blackriver1987

The screen flashed green. The file opened.

Inside was a single document. A letter, typed and formatted like something meant to be printed and mailed. I leaned closer to read it.

"'To whom it may concern,'" I read aloud. "'If you're reading this, I'm probably dead. The following information details my involvement with an organization called the Meridian Group, including names, dates, and account numbers for transactions totaling over three hundred thousand dollars. I have kept this information as insurance against any attempt on my life. A physical copy of this document, along with supporting evidence, has been hidden in a secure location. Instructions for its retrieval have been left with a trusted party, to be released to the FBI, the IRS, and every major news outlet in Colorado in the event of my death.'"

The room was silent as the implications sank in.

"The Meridian Group," Lily repeated. "That's who he stole from."

"A trusted party," Maeve said thoughtfully. "I wonder if that's true, or if he was bluffing."

"Either way, someone believed him enough to kill him anyway." I scrolled down. Names. Dates. Account numbers. A web of financial transactions that painted a picture of something much bigger than a simple con.

"This isn't just theft," Maeve said quietly. "This is organized crime. Money laundering, by the look of it."

"And Grant stumbled into the middle of it." I stared at the screen. "He didn't just steal from one person. He stole from people who make other people disappear."

"If there's a physical copy hidden somewhere," Lily said slowly, "it might be with the money. Near the falls."

"Two birds, one stone," I agreed. "We find the money, we might find the evidence too."

"No wonder he was running scared," Lily said.

"No wonder someone killed him."

We sat in silence for a moment, the weight of what we'd found settling over us. Then Atticus spoke, his voice still slightly shaky.

"What are you going to do with this?"

"Give it to Sheriff Iris," I said. "Eventually. But first..." I looked at Lily, then at Maeve. "We need to find what Grant hid near the falls. The money, and maybe that physical copy of his evidence."

"Why?" Atticus asked. "If you have the information on the laptop, why do you need the rest?"

"Because the laptop was password protected. Twice. Whoever killed Grant couldn't access any of this." I met his eyes. "But if there's a physical copy out there, something anyone could read, that's what the killer is really after. And as long as it's out there, people are in danger."

"Including you," Atticus said. "If they find out you've been looking..."

"That's a risk we have to take."

"The falls," Atticus said slowly. "Aspen Falls. That's where they found Grant's body."

"We found coordinates on the laptop," I said. "Directions to where Grant hid everything. Thirty paces from a bent pine, due east, behind loose rocks in a split boulder. But we don't know the trails the way you do."

"You know them better than anyone," Lily added. "You've been hiking out there your whole life. And now, with your gift..." She let the implication hang.

Atticus was quiet for a long moment. I could see him wrestling with the decision, weighing the risks against the desire to help.

"This isn't just a hike," Maeve said gently. "A man was killed at those falls. The people who did it are still out there, still looking for what Grant hid. If they're watching the area..."

"Then we could be walking into a trap," Atticus finished. "I understand."

"You don't have to do this," I said. "We're asking a lot."

"You are." He stood, pacing to the window and staring out at the dark street. "But Grant's body was found because of me. Because the hawk showed me where to look." He turned back to face us.

"Maybe there's a reason for that. Maybe I'm supposed to help finish this."

"Is that a yes?"

"That's a yes." He managed a small smile. "I'll meet you at the trailhead at dawn. We should go early, before anyone else is on the trails. Less chance of being seen."

"Or followed," Lily added.

"Or followed," he agreed.

"Thank you, Atticus."

"Don't thank me yet." He reached for his coat. "Let's see if we actually find anything first."

After he left, Maeve poured us all tea, her expression thoughtful.

"He's brave," she said. "Braver than he knows."

"He's terrified," Lily corrected.

"Those two things aren't mutually exclusive." Maeve handed me a cup. "Be careful tomorrow. All of you. Whoever killed Grant is still out there. And if they're watching the falls..."

"We'll be careful," I promised.

"I mean it, Alexis." Maeve's voice was unusually stern. "Albert Crane came to your café today asking questions. Martin Oakes is watching every corner of this town. And now you're planning to walk into the exact place where a murder happened, looking for evidence that people are willing to kill for." She set down her teacup. "Promise me you'll turn back at the first sign of trouble."

"I promise."

"And if you find anything, bring it straight to me. Don't go home first. Don't stop anywhere."

"Maeve, you're scaring me."

"Good." Her eyes were serious. "You should be scared. Fear keeps you sharp. Keeps you alive."

I nodded, her words settling into my bones. She was right. This wasn't a game. This wasn't just solving a mystery for the thrill of it. A man was dead, and the people who killed him wouldn't hesitate to add more bodies to the count.

But we'd come too far to stop now.

"We'll be careful," I said again. "I promise."

Maeve studied my face for a long moment, then nodded. "I'll be here when you get back. Waiting."

Tomorrow, we'd walk into the mountains, following the trail of a dead man's secrets.

And hope we didn't end up like him.

## Chapter Thirteen

The walk back from Maeve's was quiet, both of us lost in thought. We had answers now. A name. The Meridian Group. Evidence that could blow the whole thing open. And tomorrow, with Atticus's help, we might finally find what Grant had hidden.

But Maeve's warnings echoed in my mind. The danger. The people willing to kill. The promise I'd made to turn back at the first sign of trouble.

"Do you think it's really organized crime?" Lily asked as we turned onto my street. "Money laundering?"

"The numbers don't lie. Whatever Grant stumbled into, it was big. Bigger than a simple con."

"And now we're in the middle of it."

"We've been in the middle of it since Grant left his laptop at my café."

We rounded the corner, and I stopped dead.

The back door to my building was hanging open. The one that led up to my apartment.

"Alexis..." Lily grabbed my arm.

"I see it."

We approached slowly, my heart hammering against my ribs. The door hadn't just been left open. It had been forced. The frame was splintered, the lock torn from the wood.

And at the bottom of the stairs, crumpled against the railing, was Hugh.

Hugh Leland, my neighbor. He lived in the apartment above the empty shop next door, a retired widower who played his television too loud because he was hard of hearing. He always had a kind word and a wave when we passed on the stairs or the sidewalk. He had no business being caught up in any of this.

"Hugh!" I rushed to his side, dropping to my knees beside him. He was conscious but dazed, a gash on his forehead bleeding sluggishly into his white hair. "Hugh, can you hear me?"

"Alexis?" His voice was weak, confused. "Someone... I heard a noise. Came to check..."

If Hugh had heard the break-in, it must have been violent. Loud enough to penetrate walls and his diminished hearing. The thought made my stomach clench.

"Don't try to move." My hands were shaking as I pressed my sleeve against the wound, trying to slow the bleeding. "Lily, call 911."

Lily already had her phone out, her voice steady as she gave the dispatcher our address. I kept my hand on Hugh's shoulder, trying to keep him calm while guilt twisted in my stomach.

This was my fault. Someone had come looking for the laptop, and Hugh had gotten in the way. Sweet, harmless Hugh, who only wanted to help his neighbors. Who'd probably heard the commotion and come to investigate because that was the kind of man he was.

"I'm so sorry," I whispered. "Hugh, I'm so sorry."

"Not your fault," he mumbled. "Just... wrong place. Wrong time."

But it was my fault. I'd brought this danger into our building. Into his life.

Someone had broken in. Someone had hurt Hugh. And my cats...

"The cats," I breathed. "Lily, I need to check on the cats."

"Go. I'll stay with Hugh."

I took the stairs two at a time, my legs shaking beneath me. The door to my apartment was open too, the lock jimmied. I pushed through and stopped, my breath catching in my throat.

It looked like a tornado had torn through. Cushions slashed open, stuffing scattered across the floor. Drawers pulled out, contents dumped. My bookshelf had been emptied, books thrown in heaps. The kitchen cabinets hung open, dishes smashed on the counter. Every surface had been searched, every hiding place violated.

"Poppy?" My voice came out strangled. "Gus? Rocky?"

Silence.

"Sage? Millie?"

The silence stretched, terrible and absolute. My heart stopped. They couldn't be gone. They couldn't be hurt. I would never forgive myself if—

A tiny mew from somewhere in the bedroom. I followed the sound, stepping over the wreckage of my life, and found them huddled together in the back of my closet. All five of them, pressed against the wall, eyes wide with terror.

"Oh, thank god." I sank to my knees, tears spilling down my cheeks before I could stop them. "You're okay. You're all okay."

Poppy was the first to move, creeping forward to press her head against my hand. "We hid," she said, her voice smaller than I'd ever heard it. "When the door broke, we hid. Like you always told us to if there was danger."

"You did the right thing. You did exactly right."

"I wanted to fight," Rocky said, emerging from behind Gus. His orange fur was fluffed up, his eyes still wild with residual fear. "Wanted to scratch and bite. But Poppy said no. Said we had to stay hidden."

"Poppy was right." I gathered him close, feeling his racing heart against my chest. "Fighting would have gotten you hurt. Or worse."

"I was so scared," Millie whispered, still pressed against the closet wall. Her blue eyes were huge, her whole body trembling. "The noises were so loud. And then someone was in your room, tearing everything apart..."

"Come here, sweetheart." I extended my hand, and she crept forward, pressing herself against my side. "You were so brave. All of you were so brave."

Gus emerged slowly, his dignity ruffled but intact. "They were looking for something specific," he said. "Not just destroying. Searching. Methodical about it."

"Did you see them? The person who did this?"

The cats exchanged glances. It was Poppy who answered.

"Covered. Face covered with dark fabric. Hands covered with gloves. Dark clothes, dark everything. We couldn't see any features."

"What about their smell?"

Another exchange of glances. Gus shook his head slowly.

"We were too far away. Hiding in the back of the closet. And they..." He paused, searching for words. "They smelled like chemicals. Something sharp and strong, like cleaning supplies. It covered everything else."

"Intentional," Poppy added quietly. "They wanted to hide their scent. They knew someone might try to track them."

Smart. Whoever had done this had planned ahead, anticipated that cats might be able to identify them by smell. That suggested someone who knew about my gift, or at least suspected it.

"But underneath," Poppy continued, her voice dropping even lower. "Underneath the sharp smell, there was something else. Fear. And anger. So much anger, all tangled up together."

Fear and anger. That could be Albert, hunting for his evidence. It could be Dina, desperate to recover what Grant stole from her. Vernon had been detained, but I didn't know if he was still in custody or if Iris had released him. And there was Martin Oakes, the watcher, whose motives we still didn't fully understand.

Any of them could have done this. Any of them could have hurt Hugh.

Sage crept out of the closet, pressing herself against my leg. "Are we safe now?" she asked, her kitten voice trembling. "Is the bad person gone?"

"They're gone," I said, pulling her close with the others. "And I won't let them hurt you. I promise."

"We know," Poppy said. "We trust you."

The trust in her voice made the guilt twist deeper. They trusted me, and I'd put them in danger. I'd put Hugh in danger. I'd put everyone in danger by holding onto that laptop, by trying to solve this mystery myself instead of going straight to Iris.

I heard sirens in the distance, growing closer. I needed to go back downstairs, talk to the police, make sure Hugh was okay. But I couldn't bring myself to leave my cats. Not yet. Not while they were still shaking, still looking at me with those wide, frightened eyes.

"I have to go," I said finally. "The police are coming. But I'll be back soon, and I'll take you somewhere safe. I promise."

"We'll wait here," Poppy said. "In the closet. Where it's dark and hidden."

"Good. Stay there until I come back."

I made my way back downstairs on shaking legs. The ambulance had arrived, paramedics loading Hugh onto a stretcher. He was more alert now, answering their questions, though he winced when they examined the gash on his head.

"Head wounds always look worse than they are," one of the paramedics was saying. "Lots of blood vessels close to the surface. But you're going to be fine, sir."

"Alexis." Sheriff Iris was there, her expression grim. "Lily told me what happened. Are you okay?"

"I wasn't here. I was..." I hesitated. "I was at Maeve's bookshop. Lily and I both were."

"And you came back to find this."

"The back door was open. Hugh was at the bottom of the stairs." I watched the paramedics wheel him toward the ambulance. "Is he going to be okay?"

"Looks like a concussion. Maybe some stitches. But he's tough." Iris pulled out her notebook. "Did Hugh say anything about what happened? Did he see who did this?"

"Just that he heard a noise and came to check. I don't think he saw much before..." I swallowed hard. "Before they pushed him down the stairs."

"Or before he fell trying to get away." Iris looked up at the broken door, her jaw tight. "The café too?"

I hadn't even thought about the café. My stomach dropped. "I don't know. I came straight up to check on the cats."

"Let's look together."

The café was worse than my apartment. The intruder had been thorough, systematic in their destruction. Every cabinet emptied. The storage room torn apart. Even the cat room had been searched, the beds overturned, the climbing structures pulled away from the walls.

Thank goodness I didn't have any rescue cats in the café right now. The last one, a sweet tabby named Clover, had been adopted just yesterday morning. If she'd still been here during the break-in, alone and terrified...

I pushed the thought away. She wasn't here. She was safe in her new home. That was what mattered.

"They were looking for something specific," Iris said, surveying the damage. "This wasn't random vandalism. This was a search."

"The laptop." The words came out before I could stop them.

Iris turned to look at me sharply. "What laptop?"

I took a breath. This was it. The moment I'd been dreading. But there was no point in hiding it anymore. Not after this.

"Grant Granger left his laptop at my café the day he died. He never came back for it." I met her eyes, forcing myself not to look away. "I should have told you sooner. I was going to tell you tomorrow."

"You have Grant's laptop." Her voice was flat, carefully controlled.

"Had. It's not here. It's..." I hesitated, but there was no point in lying now. "It's at Maeve's. We were trying to figure out what was on it."

"You were trying to figure out—" Iris stopped herself, pressing her lips together. When she spoke again, her voice was tight with barely contained frustration. "Alexis, do you have any idea what you've done?"

"I was trying to help—"

"Albert Crane came to me three days ago asking about Grant's laptop. Asked if we'd recovered it from the cabin, if anyone had turned it in. I told him no." Her eyes were hard. "I told him we had no laptop. Because as far as I knew, we didn't."

The implication hit me like a slap. "Iris, I didn't mean to—"

"And then Dina Marsh asked the same thing. And I gave her the same answer." Iris's voice rose slightly. "I've been telling people there is no laptop. That Grant must have had it with him when he died and the killer took it. And now you're telling me it's been sitting at Maeve's bookshop this whole time?"

"Yes." The word came out small, ashamed.

"Do you understand how this makes me look? How this makes my department look?" She took a breath, visibly reining in her temper. "You've been withholding evidence in a murder investigation. Again."

"I know. I'm sorry."

"Sorry doesn't fix this." She pulled out her notebook, her movements sharp and precise. "Tell me everything. What's on the laptop. What you found. All of it."

I told her everything. The passwords. The files. The Meridian Group. The insurance letter and the possibility of physical evidence hidden near the falls. She listened without interrupting, her pen moving steadily across her notebook, her expression unreadable.

When I finished, she was quiet for a long moment.

"You cracked two passwords on a murder victim's laptop," she said finally. "How?"

I'd been dreading this question. "We... figured them out. Based on things we learned about Grant."

"You figured them out."

"Yes."

She clearly didn't believe me, but she let it go. For now.

"The Meridian Group," she said. "That's a new name. I'll need to run it through some databases, see what comes up."

"It's organized crime. Money laundering. Grant stole from them and they—"

"I'll determine what it is after I've done my own investigation." Her voice was sharp. "You've already contaminated this case enough."

I flinched. "I was trying to help."

"You were trying to solve it yourself. There's a difference." She closed her notebook with a snap. "And now someone knows you have information they want. Information they're willing to hurt people for."

I thought of Hugh, bleeding at the bottom of the stairs. Of my cats, huddled terrified in the closet.

"I know."

"You can't stay here tonight. The locks are broken, and whoever did this might come back." Iris tucked her notebook away. "Is there somewhere you can go?"

"Maeve's. Or Lily's."

"Good. Pack a bag for you and your cats. I'll have a deputy watch the building tonight, but I want you somewhere safe." She paused at the door. "And Alexis? One more thing. This search for evidence near the falls. Don't."

"But if we could find it before—"

"Don't," she repeated firmly. "Let me handle this. That's my job, not yours. After tonight, I would think you'd understand the danger you're in."

She left without waiting for a response.

Lily appeared in the doorway, her face pale. "Hugh's on his way to the hospital. They think he'll be fine, but they want to keep him overnight for observation."

"Good." I looked around at the destruction surrounding us. Broken dishes. Scattered papers. The remnants of the life I'd built here, torn apart by someone hunting for secrets. "This is my fault."

"It's not—"

"It is. I should have given Iris the laptop immediately. I should have let her handle this from the start." I picked up a broken mug, one of my favorites, hand-painted with little cats. "Instead, I played detective, and Hugh got hurt. My cats were terrorized. And now Iris thinks I've been deliberately undermining her investigation."

"You were trying to help."

"That's what I keep telling myself. But maybe I was just trying to prove I could solve it. That I was smart enough, capable enough." I set down the broken mug. "And people got hurt because of my ego."

Lily was quiet for a moment. Then she stepped closer, putting her hand on my arm.

"What are we going to do?" she asked quietly.

I thought about Iris's warning. About the danger. About Hugh's blood on the stairs and my cats' terrified eyes.

Then I thought about Grant, dead at the falls. About the Meridian Group, still operating in the shadows. About Albert Crane, searching relentlessly for evidence that could destroy him. About whoever had done this, still out there, still hunting.

If we waited for Iris to investigate the Meridian Group, to track down the evidence, to build a case... how long would that take? Days? Weeks? And in the meantime, whoever had done this would keep searching. Keep hunting. Keep hurting people who got in their way.

"We're going to do what we planned," I said. "Tomorrow morning. The falls."

"Alexis..."

"Iris is right. We're in danger. But we were already in danger the moment Grant left that laptop here. The only way out is through." I met her eyes. "We find that evidence before anyone else does. We give it to Iris. And we end this. Before anyone else gets hurt."

Lily was quiet for a long moment, searching my face. Then she nodded.

"I'll call Atticus. Make sure he still knows to meet us at dawn."

"And I'll pack a bag for me and the cats." I looked around at the destruction one more time. "We're not staying here tonight."

Upstairs, I gathered the cats into their carriers, murmuring reassurances as I worked. They went willingly, still shaken, still scared.

"Where are we going?" Sage asked, her small voice muffled by the carrier.

"Somewhere safe. Just for tonight."

"And tomorrow?"

I thought about the falls. About the money and the evidence hidden in the rocks. About whoever had done this, still out there, still hunting. About Maeve's warning to turn back at the first sign of trouble.

"Tomorrow," I said, "we will finish this."

# Chapter Fourteen

Dawn came gray and cold, the sky heavy with clouds that threatened more snow. I'd barely slept at Maeve's, my mind churning with images of my ransacked apartment, Hugh's blood on the stairs, my cats' terrified eyes.

But morning brought clarity, if not peace. We had a plan. We were going to see it through.

The cats were awake when I came downstairs, all five of them watching me with anxious eyes from their temporary beds in Maeve's warded back room. They'd been restless all night too, I could tell. Poppy's fur was slightly ruffled, and Rocky kept pacing back and forth along the edge of his blanket.

"You're going," Poppy said. It wasn't a question.

"I have to. We need to find what Grant hid before anyone else does."

"We could help." Rocky stopped pacing, his orange eyes bright with determination. "If you would let us outside. We could track scents, watch for danger, be your lookouts—"

"No, Rocky."

"But we're good at it! Remember what Gus smelled on the cold man? Remember how I found—"

"I remember. But the answer is still no." I crouched down to their level, looking at each of them in turn. "Outside is dangerous. Wolves, coyotes, mountain lions. The trail to the falls goes through wild country. I won't risk any of you."

"Inside is dangerous too," Gus said quietly. "Especially when people break in and tear our home apart."

The words hit me like a physical blow. He was right. I'd always told them that inside was safe, that the walls of the café and apartment would protect them. And then someone had smashed through those walls like they were nothing.

"You have a point," I admitted. "But no. You all stay inside. Here with Maeve, where it's safe. Her wards will protect you in ways regular walls can't."

"We don't like it," Millie said softly, her blue eyes worried. "We don't like you going into danger without us."

"I know, sweetheart. I don't like it either." I reached out and stroked her soft fur. "But Lily and Atticus will be with me. I won't be alone."

"They're not us," Sage said, pressing against my hand. "They can't hear you like we can. Can't feel when you're scared."

"I'll be careful. I promise."

Poppy stepped forward, pressing her head firmly against my palm. "Come back to us. That's all we ask. Whatever you find out there, whatever happens, come back."

"I will." I gathered them all close for a moment, feeling their warmth, their love, their fear for me. "I promise I will."

Maeve appeared in the doorway, two travel mugs of tea in her hands. "Lily's ready. And the sun's coming up."

I gave the cats one last look. "Stay here. Stay safe. I'll be back before you know it."

"We'll be waiting," Poppy said. "We'll always be waiting."

Lily and I left the cats in Maeve's care, with strict instructions to keep them in the warded back room. Maeve promised she wouldn't let them out of her sight.

The trailhead parking lot was empty when we arrived, just as I'd hoped. The sun was barely a suggestion on the horizon, the world still wrapped in that hushed stillness that comes before full daylight. Fresh snow had fallen overnight, blanketing the ground in pristine white. Our footprints would be the first to mark it.

Atticus was waiting by the trail marker, his breath pluming white in the frigid air. He looked tired but determined, a backpack slung over one shoulder and hiking poles in his hand.

"Morning," he said as we approached. "I know Lily said you were still coming, but after what happened last night... I thought you might have a change of heart."

"All the more reason to come," I said. "Whoever broke into my place was looking for what Grant hid. If we don't find it first..."

"Someone else will." He nodded grimly. "I brought supplies. Water, first aid kit, flashlight. Extra gloves in case anyone's hands get too cold. And this." He pulled a folded paper from his pocket. "I printed the coordinates you mentioned. Cross-referenced them with the trail maps I have at home."

"And?"

"The location is about a mile past the main falls. Off the marked trail, up a rocky slope." He tucked the paper away. "It's rough terrain, especially with snow on the ground. The rocks will be icy, and some of the slopes are steep. But I know a path that should get us close without too much scrambling."

"Lead the way."

We set off into the woods, Atticus in front, Lily behind him, me bringing up the rear. The trail was quiet, our footsteps muffled by the fresh powder. Above us, birds called to each other in the gray morning light, and somewhere in the distance, a woodpecker hammered against a tree.

The forest felt different in winter. Stripped of its summer greenery, the trees stood skeletal against the pale sky, their bare branches reaching upward like supplicating hands. Only the evergreens provided color, their dark needles dusted with snow. It was beautiful, in a stark and solemn way. But it was also exposed. Nowhere to hide if someone was watching.

"The hawk is nearby," Atticus said softly after we'd been walking for about ten minutes. "I can feel it. Watching us from somewhere in the trees."

"Is that good or bad?"

"Good, I think. It would warn me if there was danger ahead." He paused, tilting his head slightly, as if listening to something only he could hear. "At least, I think it would. I'm still learning to interpret what it shows me. Sometimes it's images, clear as photographs. Sometimes it's just... feelings. Impressions."

"Trust your instincts," Lily said. "That's what Maeve always tells me. The gift knows more than we do."

"Maeve said the same thing to me." A small smile crossed his face. "She also said I think too much. That I need to feel more and analyze less."

"Sounds like Maeve."

We continued on, the trail growing steeper as we climbed toward the falls. I could hear the water now, a distant roar that grew louder with each step. Even in winter, Aspen Falls never fully froze, fed by underground springs that kept the water flowing year-round. The sound was both beautiful and ominous, a constant reminder of where we were headed. Where Grant had died.

The cold was seeping through my layers despite my heavy coat, and I flexed my fingers inside my gloves to keep the circulation going. Beside me, Lily's cheeks were pink with cold, her breath coming in short puffs.

"This is where I found him," Atticus said quietly as we passed a rocky outcropping. His voice had dropped, almost reverent. "Grant. He was just... lying there. At first I thought he'd slipped, hit his head on the rocks. People underestimate how dangerous these trails can be in winter. But then I saw..."

He didn't finish. He didn't need to.

"I'm sorry you had to see that," I said.

"Me too." He took a breath, steadying himself, and kept walking. "The location you described is up ahead. Past the main viewing area, off to the east."

We left the marked trail, picking our way through scrub brush and snow-covered rocks. The terrain was treacherous, and more than once I had to grab a branch to keep from slipping. Lily stumbled behind me, and I caught her arm before she could fall.

"Careful. The rocks are icy."

"I noticed," she said dryly, but her grip on my arm was tight. "I'm more of an indoor witch, I think."

Despite everything, I almost smiled.

Atticus stopped so suddenly I nearly walked into him.

"What is it?"

He pointed ahead, his expression troubled. "Look."

I looked. And my heart sank.

The snow around the rocky slope had been trampled. Footprints everywhere, crisscrossing the area in a chaotic pattern. Some were large, heavy boots that had sunk deep into the snow. Others were smaller, lighter. At least two different people, maybe more.

"Someone's been here," Lily breathed.

"More than one someone." I moved forward carefully, trying not to disturb the tracks. "Look at the prints. Different sizes. Different treads. These are heavy work boots. These are something lighter, maybe hiking shoes."

"They were searching," Atticus said. He crouched down, examining the snow with a practiced eye. "See how the prints cluster here? And here? They were methodical. Covering the whole area section by section."

"When?" Lily asked. "How long ago?"

"Hard to say exactly. But there's fresh snow in some of the prints and not others. I'd guess they were here yesterday, maybe the day before."

I looked up at the rocky slope, my eyes scanning for the landmarks Grant had described. There. A gnarled pine tree, bent almost horizontal by years of mountain winds. And beyond it, maybe thirty paces east...

"The split boulder." I pointed. "That's where Grant said he hid it."

We made our way toward it, following the trampled path the previous searchers had left. The boulder was massive, cracked down the middle by some ancient geological force. The gap between the two halves was just wide enough for a person to squeeze through.

But the snow around it was churned to mud. The loose rocks Grant had mentioned were scattered everywhere, pulled away and discarded. Someone had been digging here. Searching. Desperate.

"They were close," Atticus said quietly. "Really close."

I squeezed into the gap between the boulders, my heart pounding. Inside, the space opened up slightly, a small hollow protected from the elements. I pulled out my phone and turned on the flashlight, sweeping the beam across the rocky interior.

Empty.

No bag. No money. No evidence.

Just bare rock and shadows.

"Anything?" Lily called from outside.

"Nothing." I backed out of the gap, my stomach heavy with disappointment. "It's empty. Either Grant never actually hid anything here, or..."

"Or someone already found it," Atticus finished.

Lily moved closer to the boulder, her expression going distant in that way I recognized. She pulled off her glove and pressed her bare hand against the cold stone.

"Lily, what are you—"

"Shh." Her eyes closed, her brow furrowing in concentration. For a long moment, she was silent, her breath misting in the cold air. Then her eyes snapped open. "No. They didn't find it."

"What do you mean? It's empty."

"I can feel their residue. Multiple people, just like we thought. Two, maybe three." She pulled her hand back, flexing her fingers against the cold. "But they left frustrated. Furious, actually. They searched everywhere. Tore the place apart. But they left empty-handed."

"Then where is it?" Atticus asked.

I looked around, really looked this time. The bent pine. The split boulder. Thirty paces east. Everything matched Grant's description. But something nagged at me. Something about the way Grant had written those directions...

Then I saw it.

About fifty yards further up the slope, partially obscured by a stand of evergreens, was another rocky outcropping. Another pine tree, bent by the wind. And at its base...

"There's another one," I breathed. "Another split boulder."

Atticus followed my gaze. "I didn't even notice. From this angle, you can't see it unless you're looking."

"Grant's directions were vague on purpose. Thirty paces from a bent pine. But there's more than one bent pine up here." I started climbing toward the second location, hope rising in my chest. "He knew someone might come looking. He wanted them to find the wrong spot first. A decoy."

The snow around the second boulder was undisturbed. Pristine white, unmarked by footprints. No one had searched here. No one had even noticed it.

My hands were shaking as I squeezed through the gap in this boulder. The space inside was similar to the first, a small protected hollow. But this time, when I swept my flashlight across the interior, the beam caught something.

A waterproof bag, wedged into a crevice near the back.

"I found it," I called, my voice cracking. "It's here."

I pulled the bag free, my heart hammering. It was heavy, heavier than I expected. I didn't open it, didn't want to risk damaging whatever was inside. But I could feel the shape of bundled papers, the solid weight of what had to be cash.

Three hundred thousand dollars. And evidence that could bring down the Meridian Group.

I squeezed back out of the boulder and held up the bag. Lily's eyes went wide. Atticus let out a long breath.

"That's it," he said. "That's really it."

"We need to go. Now." I tucked the bag inside my coat, trying to make it less obvious, but the bulge was unmistakable. "Straight to the sheriff's office. We don't stop for anything."

We made our way back down the trail faster than we'd climbed up, caution giving way to urgency. The hawk circled overhead, a dark shape against the gray sky, and I wondered if it sensed our fear. If it was watching for threats we couldn't see.

Every shadow seemed menacing now. Every sound made me flinch. Someone had already been to the falls, already searched for what we'd just found. They could still be out here. Watching. Waiting.

The parking lot came into view, and relief washed over me. Atticus's truck sat alone where we'd left it, undisturbed.

"Almost there," Lily breathed. "We made it."

We hurried across the lot toward the truck. Atticus had his keys out, was reaching for the door—

The sound of tires on gravel made us all freeze.

A black SUV turned into the parking lot, moving slowly. Deliberately. It rolled to a stop near the trailhead entrance, blocking the exit.

"Get in," Atticus said, his voice tight. "Now."

We piled into the truck, Lily and I scrambling into the back seat, the bag clutched tight against my chest. Through the window, I could see the SUV sitting there, engine idling. A figure behind the windshield, watching us.

Watching the obvious bulge under my coat.

"They saw us," Lily whispered. "They saw the bag."

Atticus started the engine and put it in gear. For a horrible moment, I thought the SUV would move to block us completely. But it stayed where it was, the figure inside making no move to get out.

"Why aren't they doing anything?" I asked.

"They're not sure," Atticus said, pulling out of the parking space and heading for the exit. "They suspect, but they're not certain. And they don't want to make a move until they know."

He had to drive past the SUV to reach the road. As we approached, I got a better look at the figure inside. Dark jacket. Face partially obscured by the sun visor. But I could feel their eyes on us, tracking our movement.

Then we were past them and turning onto the main road, the SUV pulling out behind us.

"They're following," I said, watching in the rearview mirror.

"I know." Atticus's knuckles were white on the steering wheel. "Sheriff's office is ten minutes away. We just have to make it ten minutes."

"They won't try anything on the main road," Lily said. "Too many witnesses."

"Unless they're desperate enough not to care."

The SUV stayed behind us, maintaining a steady distance. Not too close, not too far. Just... there. Watching. Waiting. Like a wolf trailing wounded prey.

"Call Iris," Atticus said. "Tell her we're coming. Tell her to meet us outside."

I fumbled for my phone, my fingers clumsy with cold and fear. The call connected on the second ring.

"Alexis? I told you not to—"

"We found it," I interrupted. "Grant's evidence. The money. We have it, and we're coming to you right now. But someone's following us. Black SUV. They saw us take it."

A pause. Then Iris's voice, sharp and professional. "How far out are you?"

"Eight minutes. Maybe less."

"I'll be waiting. Drive straight here. Don't stop for anything."

"I won't."

The line went dead. The SUV still followed, a dark shape in the mirror.

"Almost there," Atticus said, more to himself than to us. "Almost there."

The longest ten minutes of my life.

# Chapter Fifteen

The sheriff's station came into view, and I'd never been so relieved to see a building in my life. Iris was standing outside, arms crossed, her deputy Hank beside her with his hand resting on his holster.

Behind us, the black SUV slowed.

Then, as Atticus pulled into the parking lot, the SUV's engine roared. Tires squealed against the icy pavement, the back end fishtailing slightly as the driver overcorrected. They recovered quickly and accelerated down Main Street, disappearing around a corner.

"Hank, go!" Iris barked. Her deputy was already moving, sprinting toward his cruiser. Within seconds, he was pulling out of the lot, lights flashing, in pursuit.

"That them?" Iris asked as we scrambled out of the truck.

"That was them." I pulled the waterproof bag from inside my coat, my hands still shaking. "They followed us all the way from the falls."

Iris took the bag, her expression unreadable. "Get inside. All of you. Now."

We didn't argue.

The station was warm after the bitter cold of the morning, but I couldn't stop shivering. Lily sat beside me on a hard wooden bench, her shoulder pressed against mine. Atticus paced by the window, still watching the street as if the SUV might reappear at any moment.

About ten minutes later, Hank returned, shaking his head as he came through the door. "Lost them on Route 7. They turned off somewhere near the old lumber road, but by the time I got there, they'd vanished. Could have gone any of a dozen directions."

Iris nodded grimly. "Did you get a plate?"

"Partial. First three characters. I called it in, but..." He shrugged. "Could be stolen. Could be out of state. We'll see what comes back."

"All right. Get on the radio with county, give them the description. Black SUV, late model, tinted windows. Maybe someone else will spot them."

Hank headed to the back, and Iris turned her attention to the bag.

She set the bag on her desk and pulled on a pair of latex gloves. "You found this at the falls? After I specifically told you not to go?"

"Near the falls. There were two locations that matched Grant's description. The first one had been searched already. Footprints everywhere, at least two different people. But the second spot..." I took a breath. "They missed it. Grant was clever. He set up a decoy."

"Too clever for his own good, apparently." Iris unzipped the bag and began removing the contents. Bundled cash, held together with rubber bands. A thick manila envelope. A small notebook with a leather cover.

"How much?" Lily asked quietly.

Iris counted quickly, her lips moving silently. "Looks like about three hundred thousand. Give or take." She set the money aside and opened the manila envelope.

Documents. Pages and pages of documents. Bank statements showing wire transfers from multiple accounts. Records of shell companies with names like Cascade Holdings and Summit Capital Partners. Names and account numbers. A paper trail that led straight to the Meridian Group.

"This is everything," Iris murmured, flipping through the pages. "Dates, amounts, names. Transaction records going back three years." She held up one page, her eyes scanning it. "Some of these names... I recognize a few. Local businessmen. A city councilman from Denver." She set it down carefully. "This is bigger than I thought. Much bigger."

"That's why they killed him," I said. "And that's why they've been searching. They knew this was out there somewhere."

"And now they know you found it." Iris looked up at me, her expression sharp. "You realize you've made yourselves targets."

"We were already targets. They ransacked my apartment last night. Hurt my neighbor." I met her eyes. "At least now you have what you need to stop them."

Iris picked up the leather notebook and opened it. Her brow furrowed as she read. "This is a journal of some kind. Grant's handwriting, I assume." She turned a page, then another. "He was documenting everything. Names. Meetings. Conversations he overheard." She paused at one entry, her expression darkening. "He has notes here about Albert Crane. Real name Albert Kessler. Works as an 'enforcer' for the Meridian Group."

"An enforcer," Lily repeated quietly. "So, he's not Grant's college roommate."

"Definitely not." Iris kept reading. "According to this, Kessler was sent to find Grant after the money went missing. Grant spotted him in Denver three months ago and ran. That's how he ended up here."

So, Albert had been hunting Grant for months. Following him from city to city, getting closer each time, until he finally tracked him to Larkspur Valley.

"What about the others?" I asked. "Does he mention anyone else?"

Iris flipped through more pages. "There are references to someone he calls 'the accountant.' Someone inside the organization who was helping him. He doesn't use a name, just initials. D.M."

D.M. My mind raced. "Dina Marsh?"

"Possibly. Or it could be someone we haven't identified yet." Iris closed the notebook. "I'll need to go through all of this carefully. There's enough here to keep investigators busy for months."

She set everything aside and fixed me with a look I knew well. The one that said she was barely containing her frustration.

"You went to the falls," she said flatly. "After I told you not to."

"I know."

"You found crucial evidence and got followed by what I'm guessing are very dangerous people."

"I know."

"And you did all this while I was busy explaining to the state police that I had no idea my local café owner was running her own parallel investigation." Iris's voice rose slightly. "Do you have any idea the position you've put me in?"

"Iris, I'm sorry—"

"Sorry." She laughed, but there was no humor in it. "Albert Crane came to me asking about that laptop. I looked him in the eye and told him we had no laptop, that Grant must have had it on him when he died. Dina Marsh asked the same thing. I gave her the same answer." She leaned forward. "I defended your integrity to both of them. Told them if anyone in my town had found something, they would have turned it in immediately."

The shame burned in my chest. "I should have told you sooner."

"You shouldn't have needed to tell me at all. It should never have left your possession without going directly to my office." She sat back, some of the heat leaving her voice, replaced by weariness. "But what's done is done. And now I have a mess to clean up."

"The evidence—"

"The evidence is solid. I'll give you that." She glanced at the manila envelope, the notebook, the stacks of cash. "You've handed me enough to bring down a criminal organization. The question is whether I can keep you alive long enough for it to matter."

The words hung in the air, stark and sobering.

"The SUV," she said after a moment. "Did you get a look at the driver?"

"No. The windows were tinted, and they stayed in the vehicle the whole time." I hesitated. "But whoever it was, they knew exactly where to find us. They pulled into that parking lot right as we were getting into Atticus's truck. Like they'd been watching the trailhead."

"Which means they're surveilling you. Or someone told them where you'd be." Iris pulled out her notebook. "Who knew about your plan to search the falls today?"

I thought about it. "Just us. Lily, Atticus, me. And Maeve, because we stayed at her place last night."

"No one else?"

"No one."

Iris frowned. "Then either they've been following you for longer than you realized, or..."

She didn't finish the sentence. She didn't need to. The implication was clear. Someone in our circle might not be who they seemed.

"What about Vernon?" I asked. "Is he still in custody?"

"Released yesterday afternoon. We didn't have enough to hold him." She anticipated my next question. "And yes, I'm aware that means he could have been the one following you. But so could Albert Crane. Or Dina Marsh. Or Martin Oakes, that man who's been watching the town. Or any number of people connected to the Meridian Group that we haven't even identified yet."

"That SUV didn't seem like Vernon's style," I said, thinking of the hermit who lived alone in the hills. "A shiny black late-model SUV with tinted windows? Vernon strikes me more as a beat-up pickup truck kind of man."

"You're not wrong," Iris admitted. "I've seen his truck. It's older than some of my deputies." She made a note. "But that doesn't rule him out. He could have rented something. Or he could be working with someone who has access to that kind of vehicle."

"The footprints at the first site were two different sizes," Lily offered. "One set from heavy boots, large, probably a man. The other smaller, lighter. Could be two of your suspects working together."

"Or two members of the organization working in tandem." Iris made a note. "Albert and an accomplice. Or Vernon and someone else, if he's more connected to this than he's letting on."

"Vernon didn't strike me as the organized crime type," I said. "He seemed more interested in his mining claims than in money laundering."

"People surprise you." Iris closed her notebook. "I've seen mild-mannered neighbors turn out to be embezzlers. Pillars of the community running drug operations. You can never really know what someone's capable of until they're pushed."

She stood, gathering the evidence into a large paper bag. "I'm going to need official statements from all three of you. And then I'm going to need you to stay out of this."

"Iris—"

"I mean it, Alexis. You've done enough. More than enough." Her voice softened slightly. "You've given me everything I need to build a case. The laptop, the hidden evidence, the paper trail. Now let me do my job."

"And if they come after us again?"

"I'm posting a deputy outside your building. And Maeve's, if that's where you're staying." She met my eyes. "I won't let anything happen to you. But you have to trust me."

Trust. Such a simple word for such a complicated thing.

"Okay," I said finally. "We'll stay out of it."

Iris raised an eyebrow. "Why don't I believe you?"

"Because you know me."

She almost laughed at that. "Yeah. I do." She gestured toward the back room. "Hank will take your statements. And Alexis? Thank you. For bringing this in. For doing the right thing, even if you did it the wrong way."

"You're welcome. I think."

We spent the next hour giving our official statements, recounting every detail of the morning's events. Hank was thorough, asking us to repeat certain parts, clarify timelines, describe the SUV and its driver as best we could. By the time we finished, I was exhausted, running on nothing but adrenaline and cold coffee from the station's ancient machine.

"What now?" Atticus asked as we finally emerged into the late morning sunlight.

I looked up and down Main Street. No black SUV. No suspicious figures lurking in doorways. Just the quiet bustle of Larkspur Valley going about its day, oblivious to the danger that had been circling us.

And then I felt it.

That prickle at the back of my neck. That sense of being watched. But this time it wasn't the SUV or Albert Crane or anyone connected to Grant's murder. This was something else. Something older. Something that had nothing to do with criminal organizations or stolen money.

I turned slowly, scanning the street. Nothing out of place. Nothing I could point to. But the feeling persisted, that awareness of eyes on me from somewhere I couldn't see.

"Alexis?" Lily's voice was concerned. "What is it?"

"Nothing." I shook my head, trying to clear it. "Just... nerves, probably. It's been a long morning."

But it wasn't nothing. And it wasn't nerves. Whatever had been watching me in Silverpine, whatever had been testing Maeve's wards, it was still there. Still circling. Still waiting.

One problem at a time, I reminded myself. Deal with the killers first. Worry about ancient magical threats later.

"Now we wait," I said, forcing my attention back to the present. "And hope Iris can finish this before whoever's out there decides we're still a threat."

"Do you think they will?" Lily asked. "Decide we're a threat?"

I thought about the SUV, watching us from the parking lot. The figure behind the wheel, seeing us emerge with the bag. The way they'd followed us all the way to the station, only peeling away at the last moment when they saw Iris waiting with her hand near her weapon.

"I think they already have," I said. "The question is what they're going to do about it."

"They know we gave everything to Iris," Atticus said slowly. "The money, the documents, the notebook. We don't have anything they need anymore."

"But we've seen their faces. Or at least, we might have." I thought about Albert Crane, his cold eyes and practiced smile. Martin Oakes, watching from doorways. The figure in the SUV, obscured by tinted glass. "We're witnesses now. To the search, to the chase, to all of it."

"Witnesses can testify," Lily said quietly.

"Exactly."

We walked back to Atticus's truck in silence. The morning's triumph had faded, replaced by a gnawing unease. We'd found the evidence. We'd handed it over to the authorities. By all rights, our part in this should be finished.

But I couldn't shake the feeling that it was far from over.

Somewhere in Larkspur Valley, a killer was watching. Waiting. Planning.

And sooner or later, they were going to make their move.

# Chapter Sixteen

Atticus dropped us off at The Turning Page, promising to check in later. He looked as exhausted as I felt, the morning's events etched into the lines around his eyes.

"Get some rest," I told him. "And thank you. We couldn't have done this without you."

"I'm not sure I did much," he said. "But I'm glad I was there."

"You did more than you know. You found the right path. You kept us calm when that SUV showed up." I put my hand on his arm. "You were brave, Atticus. Braver than you give yourself credit for."

He ducked his head, embarrassed but pleased. "I'll check in later. Make sure you're both okay."

"We'd like that."

Lily and I watched him drive away, then slipped through the bookshop's front door. Maeve was waiting behind the counter, her silver hair loose around her shoulders, concern etched on her face.

"I felt it," she said before we could speak. "The danger. The fear. It washed over me like a wave about an hour ago. Are you both all right?"

"We're fine. We found the evidence. Gave it to Iris." I sagged against a bookshelf, the weight of the morning finally catching up to me. "But they saw us. Whoever's behind this. They followed us from the falls and watched us hand everything over to the sheriff."

"They know we found it," Lily added. "They know we're witnesses now."

Maeve nodded slowly, her expression grave. "Then you'll stay here. Both of you. Until this is resolved."

"We can't impose—"

"You're not imposing. You're family." She said it simply, as if it were the most obvious thing in the world. "Come. The cats have been asking for you every ten minutes since you left."

She led us through the bookshop, past the shelves of leather-bound volumes and the reading nooks tucked into corners. The shop itself was magical in its own quiet way, books seeming to rearrange themselves when you weren't looking, dust motes dancing in sunbeams that shouldn't have been able to reach certain corners.

We stopped at the door at the back, set into the wall so seamlessly it was almost invisible. The wood was carved with intricate patterns of vines and leaves, and if I looked closely, I could see tiny creatures hidden among them: a rabbit, a fox, an owl with knowing eyes.

Maeve pressed her palm against the center, and I felt the familiar pulse of energy as it recognized her touch and swung open.

We'd arrived so late and exhausted last night that I'd barely registered the space before collapsing into bed. Now, in the soft light of late morning, I could finally appreciate it properly.

The space opened up impossibly, larger than the building's exterior should have allowed. Much larger. What looked like a small storeroom from outside was actually a sprawling living area that defied every law of physics I knew. Warm light spilled from stained glass lamps in jewel tones of ruby, emerald, and sapphire, casting colored shadows across walls lined with tapestries depicting scenes I didn't quite recognize but felt I should.

A fire crackled in a stone hearth, the flames dancing in colors that shifted from orange to blue to green to purple. The stones around it were carved with runes that seemed to pulse gently with each flicker of the flames. Plants filled every available surface, some I recognized, like rosemary and lavender and mint, and many I didn't, their leaves in shapes and colors that seemed almost alien. They rustled gently despite the absence of any breeze, as if greeting us.

The ceiling was high and vaulted, painted with constellations that definitely moved if I looked at them too long. I watched Orion's belt shift slightly to the left, and a shooting star traced a path across the painted sky before fading. A spiral staircase in the corner led to the upper level where we'd slept, its iron railing shaped like climbing vines.

And everywhere, on shelves and windowsills and tucked into nooks, were crystals and candles and small objects that hummed with quiet power. A collection of hourglasses with sand in different colors. A set of bells that chimed softly though nothing touched them. Mirrors that reflected things that weren't quite in the room.

"I didn't notice half of this last night," Lily said, gazing up at the shifting constellations. "I was too tired to see straight."

"That's the thing about magic," Maeve said. "It reveals itself when you're ready to receive it. Last night you needed rest, so this place gave you rest. Today you need safety, so you see the protections." She gestured at the walls. "You're safe within these walls. Nothing can enter here that I haven't invited."

My cats came bounding toward me, Poppy in the lead. They'd clearly been exploring, their curiosity having overcome their earlier fear.

"You're back!" Sage announced, pressing against my ankles so hard she nearly knocked me over. "This place is amazing. There are so many smells. And the fire changes colors. And there's a cat who lives here who is very, very old and knows everything."

"Not everything," a creaky voice corrected. "Just more than most."

A large gray cat emerged from behind a cushioned armchair, moving with the slow dignity of advanced age. Her fur was the color of storm clouds, her eyes milky with cataracts, but they seemed to see right through me.

"Pearl," Maeve said fondly.

"So these are yours," Pearl said, settling onto a velvet cushion near the fire. "They've been telling me about your adventures. Foolish, but brave. The orange one wouldn't stop talking about wanting to fight the intruder."

"That's Rocky," I said. "And that sounds about right."

"He has spirit. Too much spirit and not enough caution, but that can be trained." Pearl's clouded eyes found mine. "You've stirred up quite a hornet's nest, young witch. I can smell the danger clinging to you like smoke."

"We didn't have much choice."

"There's always a choice. You chose to act rather than hide." She stretched, her old bones creaking. "I've seen your kind before. Trouble finds you whether you seek it or not. Might as well meet it head-on."

Rocky was already investigating every corner, his tail high with excitement. Gus had found a sunny spot near the fire and settled in as if he'd always belonged there. Millie was tucked behind a potted fern, watching everything with her usual wariness, but even she seemed calmer here.

"You came back," Poppy said, jumping onto the arm of the nearest chair to be closer to my eye level. "We were worried. We felt something about an hour ago. A spike of fear."

"We were being followed. But we made it to Iris in time."

"And the evidence?"

"In the sheriff's hands now. Our part is done." I stroked her fur. "Now we just have to wait for Iris to catch whoever did this."

"Waiting is hard," Millie said softly from behind her fern. "I don't like waiting."

"None of us do, sweetheart."

"Your room is still ready upstairs," Maeve said. "Rest as long as you need. I'll put together some lunch."

Before she could leave, I caught her arm. "Maeve, the watching. It's still happening. I felt it again this morning, outside the sheriff's station."

Her expression grew serious. "I know. I've felt the pressure on my wards increasing over the past few days. Whatever it is, it's growing bolder."

"But it still can't get through?"

"Not here. Not yet." She glanced at the walls, at the runes carved around the fireplace, at the crystals positioned at precise intervals along the windowsills. "My protections are strong. They've held for decades against things far worse than curious watchers. But I won't pretend I'm not concerned."

"You said before it might be residual energy from the murder. Or the ley lines reacting to tension." I searched her face. "Do you still think that's what it is?"

Maeve was quiet for a moment, and I saw Pearl's ears prick forward. "No," she said finally. "I don't. This feels intentional. Patient. Like something that's been searching for a very long time and is finally getting close to what it's looking for."

The words sent a chill down my spine. "Searching for what?"

"For you, I suspect. Or for someone like you." Maeve met my eyes, and for the first time since I'd known her, I saw real worry there. "We should talk about this properly. But not today. Today you need rest, and I need to think. When this business with the murder is resolved, we'll sit down and discuss what I've been sensing. What it might mean."

"Maeve, if I'm in danger—"

"You're in danger from the people who killed Grant Granger. That's the immediate threat. This other thing..." She shook her head. "It's patient. It's been patient for years, maybe decades. It can wait a few more days while we deal with the more pressing problem."

I wanted to argue, wanted to demand answers. But she was right. We couldn't fight on two fronts at once. And right now, the killers were the more immediate threat.

"Fine," I said. "But as soon as this is over—"

"As soon as this is over, we talk. I promise."

My phone buzzed in my pocket. I pulled it out, expecting Iris with an update. Instead, it was a text from Colton.

*I drove past the café this morning. Saw the boards on the windows. Are you okay? What happened?*

My heart clenched. I'd been so focused on the falls, the evidence, the chase, that I hadn't even thought about what the café must look like from the outside. Boarded up. Closed. A crime scene.

*I'm okay*, I typed back. *Break-in last night. Staying with a friend until it's sorted out.*

His response came almost immediately. *A break-in? Alexis, that's terrible. Do you need anything? I can come by, help clean up, whatever you need. Just say the word.*

I stared at the screen, not sure how to respond. Part of me wanted to say yes, wanted the comfort of his steady presence. But another part of me knew that pulling him into this mess would only put him in danger.

*I'm fine, really. The sheriff is handling it. I just need a few days to get things back in order.*

*If you're sure. But please, let me know if there's anything I can do. I mean it. I want to help.*

*I will. Thank you, Colton.*

*Be safe. Please. I couldn't stand it if something happened to you.*

I tucked the phone away, a complicated tangle of emotions sitting heavy in my chest. Colton's concern was real, his desire to help genuine. But there was something about his messages that felt almost suffocating. The urgency of them. The way he kept pushing even after I'd said I was fine.

Before I could even process, the phone buzzed again. Lionel this time.

*Heard about the café. I'm so sorry. Let me know if you need anything at all. No pressure, just here if you need me.*

Short. Simple. No demands, no expectations. Just Lionel being Lionel.

*Thank you*, I typed back. *That means a lot.*

He didn't respond immediately, didn't push for more information or offer again. Just let my words stand. Somehow, that felt more supportive than all of Colton's eager offers.

Another buzz. Flo.

*Alexis honey are you okay?? Mabel told me about the break-in. I'm worried sick. The girls and I are praying for you. Sunday dinner is MANDATORY when this is all over. No excuses. Love you.*

I smiled despite everything. That was pure Flo.

*I'm safe. Staying with Maeve. I'll take you up on that dinner. Love you too.*

The phone buzzed twice more in quick succession. Esther, offering to help with anything. Cordelia, asking if the cats were all right and offering to knit them "comfort blankets for their trauma." Even Gabe from the hardware store, saying he could help board up the windows better if needed.

"Popular today," Lily observed, watching my phone light up again.

"Small town." I silenced the phone and set it on a side table. "Word travels fast."

"They care about you. That's not a bad thing."

"I know. It's just..." I shook my head. "A lot. All at once."

"Colton?" Lily asked, having watched me cycle through the messages.

"And Lionel. And Flo. And half the town, apparently."

"That's sweet."

"It is." I sank into an armchair that seemed to mold itself around me, impossibly comfortable. "They're all good people."

"But?"

I thought about the question. About Colton with his steady warmth and easy affection. About the way he always seemed to be reaching for me, always touching, always making sure everyone knew we were together. He wanted to take care of me. Wanted to fix things for me. Wanted to be the one I turned to in a crisis.

And then I thought about Lionel. Patient Lionel, who never pushed, who was simply there whenever I needed him. Who made space for me without demanding anything in return. Who trusted me to know what I needed and ask for it if I wanted help. Even his text had been different. *No pressure, just here if you need me.*

Two different kinds of care. Two different ways of loving someone.

"I don't know," I said finally. "Everything's so complicated right now. I can't think about any of that until this is over."

"Fair enough." Lily settled into the chair beside me, pulling a knitted blanket over her lap. "But when this is over..."

"When this is over, I'll figure it out. I promise."

Poppy jumped into my lap, circling twice before settling down. "You're safe here," she said. "I can feel it. The walls hum with protection. Like a heartbeat."

"Maeve's wards."

"More than wards. This place is loved. That's the strongest magic of all." She kneaded my leg gently with her paws. "Rest now. You've been running on fear and adrenaline all morning. Let yourself stop."

She was right. I stroked her fur, letting the warmth of the fire and the safety of Maeve's home seep into my bones. For the first time since finding the ransacked apartment, I felt myself begin to relax.

The café was closed. My apartment was a crime scene. A killer was still out there, hunting for loose ends. And something ancient and patient was watching from beyond the wards, waiting for a chance to reach me.

But for now, in this moment, we were safe.

Maeve returned with a tray of sandwiches and tea, setting it on a low table between us. "Eat. Rest. There's nothing more you can do today."

"What about Iris? The investigation?"

"Will continue without you. That's what you wanted, isn't it? To hand over the evidence and let the authorities handle it?"

"I guess."

Maeve sat across from us, Pearl immediately climbing into her lap with the slow deliberation of age. "You've done your part, Alexis. More than your part. Now you need to trust that justice will follow."

Trust. There was that word again.

"What if it doesn't?" I asked. "What if they can't catch whoever did this?"

"Then we'll deal with that when it comes." Maeve's eyes met mine, steady and sure. "But borrowing trouble from tomorrow won't help you rest today."

She was right. I knew she was right.

I picked up a sandwich and took a bite, surprised to find I was actually hungry. The fire crackled, shifting from blue to green. The cats dozed in various spots around the room, finally relaxed. Pearl and Poppy had started some kind of silent conversation, the older cat occasionally twitching an ear in response to something only they could hear.

And slowly, gradually, the tension in my shoulders began to ease.

Tomorrow would bring whatever it brought.

But today, we were safe.

And that would have to be enough.

# Chapter Seventeen

I slept better than I had any right to, wrapped in Maeve's wards and the comfort of knowing we'd done everything we could. The cats had piled onto the bed with me, a warm, furry weight that anchored me through the night. Poppy claimed the pillow beside my head, Gus stretched along my feet, Rocky curled against my back, and Millie and Sage wedged themselves into whatever spaces remained.

Wednesday morning came soft and gray, snow falling gently outside the window. I lay there for a moment, listening to the quiet, watching the flakes drift past the glass. For just a few seconds, I could pretend everything was normal. That I'd wake up, go downstairs to my café, and start another ordinary day.

Then my phone buzzed on the nightstand, and reality came crashing back.

Iris.

"Good morning," I answered, sitting up carefully so as not to disturb Sage, who was curled against my hip.

"Morning. I have an update. Can you come down to the station?"

"Actually, I was hoping to check on my apartment and the café today. See what kind of damage I'm dealing with."

A pause. "I can meet you there. But do not go inside without me or a deputy with you. Understood?"

"Understood."

"Give me an hour. I'll meet you at the café."

I woke Lily, and we got ready quietly, not wanting to disturb Maeve, who I suspected had been up late reinforcing her wards. The cats were less cooperative, all of them wanting to come along.

"It's not safe yet," I told Poppy firmly. "You stay here where you're protected."

"We could help," Rocky insisted, his tail lashing with frustration. "We could sniff out danger. Watch for threats. Be useful."

"You are useful. Here. Keeping each other safe."

"That's not the same and you know it." He fixed me with those intense orange eyes. "We're supposed to protect you. That's our job."

"Your job is to stay alive. That's the only job I care about right now."

"You could also get hurt," Gus added, his deep voice unusually gentle. "Or lost. Or worse. The world outside these wards is dangerous right now, Rocky. Even for brave cats."

Rocky's fur settled slightly, though he still looked unhappy. "I don't like it."

"None of us do," Poppy said. She pressed her head against my hand. "But she's right. We stay here. We wait. And when she comes back, we'll be here."

"Please," I said, scratching behind Rocky's ears. "Stay with Maeve. I'll be back soon. I promise."

Rocky finally relented, herding the others away from the door with a look that promised we'd discuss this later. Millie's worried blue eyes followed me all the way out.

The walk to the café was strange. Familiar streets, familiar buildings, but everything felt different now. Tainted somehow. I kept scanning the faces of passersby, looking for threats that might not be there. Every dark SUV made my heart jump. Every stranger who glanced my way felt like a potential enemy.

Iris was already waiting when we arrived, her cruiser parked in front of the boarded-up windows. Deputy Hank stood by the door, looking cold but alert, his breath misting in the frigid air.

"How's Hugh?" I asked before anything else.

"Released from the hospital yesterday. Mild concussion, six stitches. He's tough." Iris gestured toward the door. "Ready to go in?"

I wasn't. But I nodded anyway.

The café looked worse in daylight than it had in the chaos of Monday night. The destruction was thorough, methodical. Every drawer emptied, every cabinet opened. The storage room was a mess of scattered supplies, broken jars, spilled coffee beans that crunched under our feet. Even the cat room had been torn apart, every hiding spot the cats loved exposed and violated.

I bent down and picked up one of Rocky's favorite toys, a catnip mouse that had been stepped on and flattened. Such a small thing. But it made my throat tight.

"They were looking for something specific," Iris said, echoing what she'd said two nights ago. "Not random vandalism."

"The laptop. They thought I still had it."

"Probably." She pulled out her notebook. "Let's talk upstairs."

My apartment was worse. More personal. My books scattered across the floor, pages torn from some of my favorites. My clothes pulled from the closet and thrown in heaps. The mattress slashed open, stuffing everywhere like snow that had fallen indoors. Even my small box of keepsakes had been dumped out, old photographs and trinkets trampled underfoot.

I bent down and picked up a photo of my mother. The frame was cracked, glass splintered, but the picture was intact. She smiled up at me from twenty years ago, young and vibrant, before the illness took her.

"I'm sorry," Iris said quietly. "I know this is hard to see."

"It's just stuff." My voice came out steadier than I felt. "It can be replaced."

But it wasn't just stuff. It was my home. My sanctuary. The life I'd built here, piece by piece, after leaving everything else behind. And someone had violated it completely. Touched everything I owned. Destroyed things just for the sake of destruction.

"You said you had an update," Lily said, steering us back to business. I was grateful for the redirect.

Iris nodded, flipping open her notebook. "We've made progress. Martin Oakes, the man who's been watching the town? We finally got him to talk."

"And?"

"He's a private investigator. Licensed out of Denver." Iris flipped a page. "He was hired by the family of one of Grant's victims, a woman named Opal Finch. They wanted him to track Grant down and recover whatever money he could."

I remembered that name from Grant's spreadsheet. Opal Finch. Sixty-five thousand dollars. And Grant's cruel note: "Widow. Lonely. Desperate for connection. Easy."

"He's been following Grant's trail for months," Iris continued. "Finally tracked him here about a week before the murder. He was still gathering information, trying to figure out where Grant had hidden the money, when Grant turned up dead."

"So, he's not connected to the killing?"

"Solid alibi. He was in Silverpine the morning Grant was killed, caught on security camera at a gas station. Timestamped." Iris flipped a page. "He's been cooperative. Embarrassed, actually. Said he's been doing this work for twenty years and never had a case go this sideways."

"Why is he still in town?" Lily asked. "If Grant's dead and he didn't kill him, why stick around?"

"The money." Iris shrugged. "His client hired him to recover it, not just find Grant. When Grant turned up dead, Oakes figured the money was still out there somewhere. He stayed hoping someone would find it, or that he might be able to track it down himself. He wanted to see the case through, bring something back to the Finch family besides bad news." She made a note. "Now that we've recovered the funds, he's agreed to stay in town a few more days in case we have follow-up questions. After that, he'll head back to Denver and close out the case with his clients."

"So at least they'll get their money back," I said.

"Eventually. Once it's processed as evidence and the case is closed, it'll be returned to the victims. All of them, not just the Finches." Iris almost smiled. "Small consolation, but it's something."

"That explains why he was watching," Lily said. "But not who killed Grant."

"No. But it narrows things down." Iris flipped another page. "Vernon Holt has been cleared as well."

"Really?" I hadn't expected that.

"His story about finding the cabin already ransacked checked out. We found a witness, a hiker who saw Vernon on the trail that evening, headed toward his own property, not the cabin. And for the morning of the murder, he was at the hardware store in Millbrook, buying supplies. Gabe confirmed the timing."

"So, Vernon really was just in the wrong place at the wrong time."

"Looks that way. He's cantankerous and territorial, but he's not a killer." Iris almost smiled. "He did say to tell you he's sorry about your café. Said he knows what it's like to have your home violated."

That was unexpectedly kind, coming from Vernon. Maybe there was more to the old hermit than I'd thought.

"That leaves Dina and Albert," Lily said.

Iris's expression shifted. Something guarded crept into her eyes. "That's where it gets complicated."

"Complicated how?"

"Dina Marsh." Iris tapped her pen against the notebook. "She presented herself as a victim. One of Grant's marks. And she was. He did steal forty thousand dollars from her."

"But?"

"But when we dug deeper into her background, we found connections to the Meridian Group. Financial transactions that link her to some of their shell companies." Iris shook her head. "We're still unclear how, exactly. She might be an investor who got burned. She might be something more. But she's not just a woman scorned."

"She could have been working with Grant," I said slowly, the pieces rearranging in my mind. "Or working for the people Grant stole from. Maybe both."

"Either is possible. We're still investigating."

"And Albert?"

Iris's jaw tightened. "I checked both names. Albert Crane and Albert Kessler, the name from Grant's notebook. Neither one turns up anything real."

"Nothing?"

"Ghost records. The kind you buy when you need a new identity fast. No employment history before five years ago. No credit history. No family, no school records, no paper trail of any kind." She closed her notebook. "I ran both names through every database I have access to. State, federal, even called in a favor with a friend at the FBI. Albert Crane and Albert Kessler are both fake identities. Whoever this man really is, he's gone to a lot of trouble to make sure no one can find out."

"An enforcer," Lily said. "That's what Grant called him in his notes. Someone sent to clean up messes."

"That fits with what we're seeing. Professional. Thorough. Patient." Iris met my eyes. "And very, very dangerous."

"The footprints at the falls," Lily added. "Two different sizes. Two people working together."

"We noticed. And yes, that's exactly what we're thinking." Iris pocketed her notebook. "Dina and Albert. We don't have proof yet, but they're our primary suspects. Both of them."

"Have you brought them in for questioning?"

"Dina's been cooperative. Answered all our questions, provided documentation for her whereabouts. Some of it checks out, some of it doesn't." Iris's jaw tightened. "Albert is a different story. He checked out of the Pine Lodge yesterday. Left no forwarding address."

My stomach dropped. "He's gone?"

"From the lodge, yes. But his SUV was spotted on Route 7 this morning, heading toward town." She gave me a hard look. "He hasn't left the area. Which means he's still here for a reason."

"The evidence. He knows we found it. He knows it's with you now."

"And he knows you're the one who found it." Iris headed for the stairs. "Which is why I'm keeping a deputy on you until this is resolved. Hank will be outside Maeve's place tonight."

"You think he'll come after us?"

"I think desperate people do desperate things. And Albert, whoever he really is, has been very desperate to find what Grant hid." She paused at the top of the stairs. "Stay at Maeve's. Stay together. And if you see Albert or Dina, call me immediately. Don't engage."

"And if they engage with us?"

"Then you run. You hide. And you call me." Her voice was firm. "These aren't amateurs, Alexis. These are people who've killed before and won't hesitate to do it again. Promise me you won't try to handle this yourself."

"I promise."

She studied my face for a moment, as if checking whether I meant it. Then she nodded and headed down the stairs.

We followed her down, past the wreckage of my café, out into the cold gray morning. My phone buzzed with a text from Colton.

*Thinking about you. Any news?*

I typed back quickly: *Meeting with Iris now. Will update you later.*

*Be careful. Please.*

Another buzz, this one from Lionel: *Saw Iris's cruiser outside your place. Everything okay?*

*Just checking on the damage. I'm fine.*

*Good. Let me know if you need anything.*

Short, simple, no pressure. Even now, in the middle of everything, the contrast between them was stark.

"What about the café?" I asked Iris as she unlocked her cruiser. "Can I start cleaning up?"

"Give me another day. We're still processing some evidence." Her expression softened slightly. "But after that, yes. I'll let you know when you can start putting things back together."

Putting things back together. Such simple words for such an impossible task.

Lily and I watched Iris drive away, then stood in silence for a moment, staring at the boarded windows of The Cozy Purrch.

"Two suspects," Lily said finally. "Dina and Albert. Working together."

"Maybe. We still don't know for sure."

"But it makes sense. The footprints. The way they've both been circling, asking questions. Dina playing the victim while Albert played the grieving friend." She pulled her coat tighter against the cold. "The question is what they'll do now that the evidence is out of reach."

I thought about Albert's cold eyes. About Dina's barely contained fury beneath her polished exterior. About the SUV that had followed us from the falls, watching, waiting.

"Nothing good," I said. "Nothing good at all."

## Chapter Eighteen

The walk back to Maeve's felt longer than it should have. Every shadow seemed to hold a threat. Every passing car made me flinch. A black pickup truck rumbled past, and I grabbed Lily's arm before I could stop myself.

"It's not them," she said quietly. "Just a truck."

"I know. I'm sorry."

"Don't be. I'm jumping at shadows too."

By the time we slipped through the bookshop door, my nerves were frayed to breaking. The familiar smell of old books and dried herbs washed over me, usually so comforting, but today it barely registered.

"Well?" Maeve asked, emerging from behind the counter. She took one look at our faces and her expression shifted to concern. "That bad?"

"Two suspects cleared. Two remaining." I gave her the summary as we made our way to the back, past the shelves that seemed to lean in to listen. "Martin Oakes was a PI hired by one of Grant's victims. Vernon was just in the wrong place at the wrong time. But Dina has ties to the Meridian Group, deeper than she let on. And Albert's disappeared from the lodge but is still in town somewhere."

"And the evidence?"

"Safe with Iris. For whatever good it does us now." I paused at the carved door. "The killer knows we found it. Knows we're the ones who turned it in. Iris has a deputy watching us, but..."

"But determined people find ways," Maeve finished. She pressed her palm to the door, and it swung open. "Come. You need rest. And I need to think."

The cats swarmed us the moment we entered Maeve's home, Sage climbing my leg before I could even take off my coat.

"You were gone too long," she complained. "We were worried. Pearl told us stories to pass the time, but it wasn't the same."

"I'm sorry. I'm here now."

Poppy circled my ankles, then jumped onto the arm of the nearest chair to look me in the eye. "You smell like fear. And sadness. What happened?"

"I saw the café. And my apartment." I swallowed hard. "It's bad, Poppy. Everything's destroyed."

"Things can be replaced," she said, echoing what I'd told Iris. But her voice was gentle, not dismissive. "You can't be replaced. That's what matters."

Rocky bounded over, his tail high but his eyes worried. "Did you find the bad people? Are they caught?"

"Not yet. But the sheriff knows who they are now. She's looking for them."

"Then why do you still smell afraid?"

Because they're still out there. Because they know where I am. Because a deputy with a gun might not be enough to stop people who've already killed once.

"Because it's not over yet," I said. "But it will be soon. One way or another."

Gus had risen from his spot by the fire to greet me, pressing his solid weight against my legs. "We're here," he said simply. "Whatever happens, we're here."

The rest of the day crawled by like honey in winter. I tried to read, but the words blurred together, my eyes skipping over the same paragraph three times without absorbing a single sentence. I tried to nap, but every time I closed my eyes, I saw my ransacked apartment, my mother's cracked photo frame, Rocky's flattened toy. Tried to help Maeve with inventory in the book shop, but my hands wouldn't stop shaking, and I dropped a ceramic bowl that shattered across the floor.

"Enough," Maeve said gently, taking the dustpan from my trembling fingers. "Go sit. Let the fire warm you. There's nothing that needs doing right now except waiting."

But waiting was the hardest thing of all.

Lily wasn't faring much better. She paced the length of Maeve's living room, back and forth, back and forth, her boots wearing a path across the ancient rug. Her fingers kept twitching, reaching for something to do, some way to be useful.

"You're making me dizzy," Gus said from his spot by the fire after the twentieth pass. "Tell her to sit down. Rest. She's wearing out my eyes."

"Gus says you're making him dizzy," I told Lily. "He wants you to sit down."

"I can't rest. Not while they're still out there." She paused at the window, peering through a gap in the curtains at the street below. "Every car that passes, I think it's them. Every person who walks by..."

"He also says wearing a hole in the floor won't catch them any faster."

Lily stopped pacing long enough to shoot Gus a look. "Tell him I'll rest when this is over."

"She says—"

"I heard her." Gus put his head back on his paws. "Humans. Always thinking movement equals progress."

By late afternoon, the tension had become almost unbearable. The cats were restless, picking up on our anxiety, unable to settle in any one spot for long. Rocky kept prowling the perimeter of the room, checking the windows and doors as if he could guard them himself. Millie had wedged herself into the smallest corner she could find, her blue eyes huge and frightened. Even Pearl, ancient and usually unflappable, had retreated to a high shelf, her milky eyes tracking every movement.

"Something's wrong," Poppy said, appearing at my side. Her calico fur was slightly puffed, her ears swiveling. "The air feels heavy. Like before a storm."

"It's just nerves."

"No." She shook her head firmly. "It's more than that. Something's coming. I can feel it pressing against my whiskers."

And underneath that feeling, something else. Something I'd almost forgotten in the chaos of murders and evidence and desperate criminals.

The watching.

It was there, at the edge of my awareness. That ancient, patient presence I'd felt in Silverpine and outside the sheriff's station. Still circling. Still waiting. But somehow... different tonight. Closer. More attentive.

As if it too sensed something was about to happen.

Maeve had been quiet most of the day, moving through her home with a distracted air, pausing occasionally to touch the walls or murmur words I couldn't quite hear. Now she stopped in the middle of the room, her head tilted as if listening to something none of us could hear.

"The wards are restless," she said softly. "Something's pressing against them. Testing."

"The watching?" I asked. "The thing we talked about before?"

"No. This is different. Cruder." Her silver brows drew together. "The other presence is still there, at the edges. Observing. But this... this is someone physically probing my defenses. Looking for weaknesses."

"Human, then. Not magical."

"Human intent, at least. Though they've found something to help them." She moved to the window, pulling aside the curtain to peer out at the darkening street. "I can feel them trying different approaches. The front door. The back. The windows. They're methodical."

My blood went cold. "Can they get through?"

"Not easily. These wards have held for decades against things far worse than curious criminals." But her voice held a note of uncertainty I'd never heard before. "Still... I should reinforce them. Just in case."

She disappeared into her workroom, and I heard her voice rise in a soft chant, words in a language that predated English by centuries. The walls seemed to shimmer briefly, the runes around the fireplace glowing brighter for a moment before settling back to their usual subtle pulse.

When she emerged, her face was pale but determined. "That's the best I can do. The wards will hold against magical assault indefinitely. But if someone decides to simply break down the door with brute force..." She spread her hands. "Magic has its limits."

Lily and I exchanged a look. Brute force was exactly what we were afraid of.

The sun set early, winter stealing the light before five o'clock. The windows went dark, and Maeve lit candles and lamps, filling the space with warm golden light. But it felt like putting a bandage on a wound that needed stitches.

We ate dinner without tasting it, spoke without really saying anything. Hank was outside, I reminded myself. A trained deputy, armed and alert. I'd seen him when I checked earlier, sitting in his cruiser with the engine running for heat, his eyes scanning the street. And Maeve's wards were strong.

But none of that stopped the dread from pooling in my stomach.

"We should try to sleep," Lily said around nine. "Whatever happens, we'll need our strength."

"You go ahead. I'll be up soon."

She climbed the spiral staircase, her footsteps echoing in the quiet. I heard her moving around in the room above, then the creak of the bed as she lay down.

I couldn't follow her. Couldn't close my eyes and pretend everything was fine. So I sat in the armchair by the dying fire, watching the flames shift from blue to green to orange, and tried not to think about all the ways this night could go wrong.

The cats had settled into an uneasy rest, scattered around the room in their usual spots but with ears pricked, ready to wake at the slightest sound. Poppy was curled on the ottoman near my feet. Gus lay by the hearth. Rocky had positioned himself by the back door, self-appointed guardian. Millie and Sage were tucked together in a basket near the bookshelf.

The house was quiet. Too quiet. Even the usual creaks and settles of an old building had gone silent, as if the whole structure was holding its breath.

My phone buzzed. I nearly jumped out of my skin.

A text from an unknown number.

*We need to talk. Meet me outside. Come alone.*

My heart hammered against my ribs. I stared at the screen, reading the words over and over, as if they might rearrange themselves into something less ominous.

Another buzz.

*I know who killed Grant. But I can't go to the police. They'll arrest me too. Please. I just want this to be over.*

I should wake Lily. Call Iris. Do anything except what the message was asking.

But something about the words nagged at me. The desperation. The fear.

*Who is this?* I typed back.

The response came immediately.

*Dina. I know you don't trust me. But Albert is dangerous. More dangerous than you know. He's planning something tonight. I can help you stop him, but you have to come now. Before it's too late.*

I stood up, my legs unsteady. Through the window, I could see the dark shape of Hank's cruiser parked at the curb. Snowflakes drifted lazily through the glow of the streetlamp. Everything looked peaceful. Normal.

But nothing about this was normal.

Another buzz.

*Please. I'm across the street. In the alley beside the hardware store. Five minutes. That's all I'm asking.*

Every instinct screamed at me to ignore it. To stay inside where it was safe. To let Iris handle whatever was happening.

But if Dina was telling the truth, if Albert was planning something tonight...

"Don't."

I spun around. Poppy was sitting at my feet, her eyes gleaming in the firelight. She must have woken when my phone buzzed, padding over silently while I stared at the screen.

"Don't go out there," she said. "It's a trap."

"You don't know that."

"I know how fear smells. And that message reeks of it. But not her fear." Her tail lashed once, hard. "Yours. They want you scared. They want you to make a mistake."

"What if she's telling the truth? What if Albert really is—"

"Then tell the deputy. Tell the sheriff. Tell anyone except yourself." Poppy stood, placing her paws on my knee, her eyes boring into mine. "You're not a hero, Alexis. You're a woman who talks to cats and makes good coffee. Let the people with guns handle the dangerous parts."

"But—"

"No buts." Her voice was fierce now, fiercer than I'd ever heard it. "You've already done more than anyone could ask. You found the evidence. You gave it to the authorities. Your job is done. Now your job is to stay alive so you can open your café again and take care of us and live your life." Her claws pricked gently through my pants. "Don't throw that away for someone who might be lying to lure you outside."

I looked at the phone in my hand. At the message glowing on the screen.

*Two minutes*, came another text. *Please. He's going to kill again. I can't let that happen.*

"Poppy..."

"No." Her voice was firm. "Wake Lily. Wake Maeve. Show them the messages. But do not go outside."

She was right. I knew she was right.

I turned toward the staircase, ready to wake Lily, ready to do the sensible thing for once in my life.

And that's when the lights went out.

All of them. The fire in the hearth. The stained glass lamps. Even the soft glow of Maeve's crystals. Everything plunged into darkness so complete I couldn't see my own hand in front of my face.

The cats erupted into chaos, yowling and hissing.

"The door!" Poppy screamed. "Someone's breaking down the door!"

A crash from somewhere outside. Glass shattering. Then a sound I recognized with horrible clarity.

A gunshot.

And then another.

"Lily!" I screamed, stumbling toward the stairs in the darkness. "Maeve!"

But before I could reach them, something hit the back door. Once. Twice. On the third impact, the wood splintered.

And cold air rushed in, carrying with it the smell of snow and smoke and something else.

Something that smelled like death.

## Chapter Nineteen

I couldn't see. Couldn't think. The darkness was absolute, pressing against me like a physical weight.

"Alexis!" Lily's voice from somewhere above me, on the stairs. "What's happening?"

"Stay up there! Someone's breaking in!"

The cats were crying out in the darkness, their voices overlapping in panic.

"I can't see!" Sage wailed. "Why can't I see?"

"Stay together!" Poppy commanded. "Everyone stay together!"

Another crash against the back door. The wood groaned, splintered further. One more hit and it would give way completely.

Then Maeve's voice, calm and clear despite the chaos. Words I didn't recognize, ancient and resonant, spoken with the weight of decades of practice. The syllables seemed to hang in the air, vibrating with power.

Light bloomed in the darkness. Not the warm glow of lamps or fire, but something else. A pale silver luminescence that seemed to emanate from the walls themselves, from the very bones of the house. It was cold light, moonlight captured and held, and it revealed everything in stark relief.

I could see again. The cats were clustered near the fireplace, ears flat, fur bristled, a tight knot of terrified animals trying to protect each other. Lily was halfway down the stairs, her face pale in the strange light, her hand gripping the iron railing so hard her knuckles were white. And Maeve stood in the center of the room, her arms raised, her silver hair floating around her as if caught in an unfelt wind.

"The wards are holding," she said through gritted teeth. "But they're meant to protect against magical threats. Against things that creep through shadows and dreams. If someone is using brute force..."

"That's impossible," Lily said. "Who could—"

The back door exploded inward.

Cold air rushed through the opening, carrying snowflakes and the acrid smell of smoke. And in the doorway stood a figure I recognized.

Dina Marsh.

But not the Dina I'd met before. Not the polished, grieving victim with her designer clothes and careful composure. This Dina's eyes were hard, her face twisted with fury. Her hair was wild, her coat torn. In her hand, she held a gun.

"Hello, Alexis," she said, stepping over the threshold. "We need to talk."

"Dina, wait—"

"Shut up." She raised the gun, pointing it directly at my chest. The barrel was steady. She'd done this before. "Where is it? The evidence. The documents. Where did you hide them?"

"They're with the sheriff. I gave them to Iris. It's over."

"It's not over!" Her voice cracked, desperation bleeding through the fury. "Those documents have my name on them. My accounts. Everything that ties me to the Meridian Group. If they go public, I'm finished. Prison for the rest of my life, if I'm lucky. And if I'm not lucky..." She laughed bitterly. "The Meridian Group doesn't let witnesses survive to testify."

"You were working with them," I said, the pieces finally clicking into place. "You weren't just one of Grant's victims. You were part of the operation."

"I was their accountant." She took another step into the room, the gun never wavering. "Moved their money, cleaned their books, made it all look legitimate. Twenty million dollars over five years, flowing through shell companies and offshore accounts. And then Grant figured it out. Stupid, greedy Grant. He stole three hundred thousand dollars and threatened to expose everything if they came after him."

"So, you killed him."

"No." Her jaw tightened. "That wasn't me."

A second figure stepped through the ruined doorway. Albert Crane. Kessler. Whatever his real name was. His cold eyes caught the silver light, and he held a gun in his hand as well. Snow dusted his dark coat, and there was something dark on his gloves. Something that looked like blood.

"That was me," he said calmly. "Grant was a loose end. I don't like loose ends."

My blood turned to ice. Two of them. Two guns. And we were trapped.

"The deputy outside," I managed. "The gunshots—"

"Dead." Albert said it flatly, without emotion. "Two shots, center mass. He went down before he could even draw his weapon." He moved further into the room, his gaze sweeping over Maeve, Lily, the cats. "Interesting place. All those locks and wards and magical protections, but a solid boot still breaks down a door. Funny how that works."

Wards. Magical protections. The words landed wrong, too specific, too knowing. How did a financial criminal know what wards were? I filed the question away, because right now had a more immediate problem.

Maeve's arms lowered slowly, the silver light dimming but not fading entirely. Her wards protected against magical intrusion, against things that crept through shadows and dreams. But two people with guns and determination? That was a different kind of threat entirely.

"What do you want?" I asked, trying to keep my voice steady. "The evidence is gone. You can't get it back."

"We want a chance," Dina said. "A head start. Enough time to disappear before those documents make it to the FBI." She gestured with the gun. "You're going to call the sheriff. Tell her you made a mistake. Tell her the documents were fake, planted by someone trying to frame innocent people. Buy us time to get out of the country."

"She won't believe that."

"She will if you're convincing enough." Dina's smile was brittle, desperate. "And you'll be very convincing. Because if you're not..."

"Enough talking," Albert snapped. "The documents. The originals. How do we get them back?"

"You can't," I said. "They're evidence in a murder investigation. Iris has already sent copies to the state police. Even if you kill all of us, it won't change anything."

Dina's face contorted. For a moment, I thought she might pull the trigger right then. But Albert raised a hand, stopping her.

"She's lying," he said. "Trying to buy time. The sheriff is competent, but she's not that fast. Small-town bureaucracy moves slowly." He turned those cold eyes on me. "You have until the count of three to tell us where the original documents are. After that, I start with the cats."

"No!" The word ripped out of me before I could stop it.

Rocky snarled from his position near the fireplace. "Let him try. I'll take his eyes out."

"Rocky, don't," Poppy warned, but her voice was shaking. "Stay still. Stay quiet."

"One," Albert said.

"The documents are gone," I insisted. "There's nothing you can do—"

"Two."

Albert raised his gun, pointing it at the cluster of cats. Sage pressed herself against Poppy, trembling so hard I could see it from across the room. Millie had gone completely still, frozen with terror. Even Gus, brave stoic Gus, had positioned himself in front of the others, ready to take the first bullet.

"Wait!" The word tore out of me. "Wait, please. I'll tell you. Just don't hurt them."

Albert smiled, a cold expression that never reached his eyes. "I knew you'd be reasonable."

I took a breath, my mind racing. I needed to buy time. Needed to think of something, anything, to get us out of this.

And then I felt it.

A presence at the edge of my awareness. Not human. Not cat. Something else. Something with wings and sharp eyes and a fierce, wild intelligence.

The hawk.

Atticus.

I didn't know how I knew, but I knew. He was out there somewhere, watching through the hawk's eyes. Seeing what was happening. Maybe he'd heard the gunshots. Maybe he'd felt something was wrong. It didn't matter. He was there.

"The documents," I said slowly, "are in a safe. In the back room of the bookshop. Behind the counter. Maeve keeps the combination in her head."

It was a lie, and not even a convincing one. But I needed them to move. Needed them away from the cats, away from Lily and Maeve.

"Show me," Albert said, gesturing with his gun. "Now."

"I'll go with her," Dina said. "You stay here. Watch the others."

"No." Albert's voice was sharp. "I don't trust her. She's proven she's clever. I'll handle this myself." He grabbed my arm, his grip bruising. "Move."

I moved toward the door that led to the bookshop, my legs shaking. Behind me, I heard Dina ordering Lily and Maeve to sit down, to put their hands where she could see them. Heard Poppy's voice, low and urgent, telling the other cats to be ready.

Ready for what, I didn't know.

The bookshop was dark, the silver light from Maeve's spell not extending this far. I fumbled for the counter, my hands trembling against the wood.

"Hurry up," Albert said, pressing the gun against my spine. "I'm not a patient man."

"I'm trying. It's dark—"

Glass shattered overhead. Something massive crashed through the skylight, a blur of wings and talons and fury.

The hawk.

It dove straight at Albert's face, screaming, claws raking across his eyes. He stumbled backward, firing blindly, the shot going wide and shattering a shelf of books. I dropped to the floor, covering my head as the hawk wheeled and struck again, relentless, savage.

From the back room, I heard shouting. Dina's voice, high and panicked. Then another sound, a sound I recognized.

Cats.

All of them. Rocky leading the charge, a streak of orange fury launching himself at Dina's legs. "For my family!" he screamed, claws extended, teeth bared.

Gus was right behind him, silent and deadly, going for the hand that held the gun. Even Millie, shy, skittish Millie, was hissing and spitting like a demon, darting at Dina's face.

"Get them off!" Dina screamed, her gun going off, the shot hitting the ceiling. Plaster rained down. She tried to kick Rocky away, but Poppy was there now, teeth sinking into her ankle with all the force her small body could muster.

"You threatened our person!" Poppy snarled around the mouthful of flesh. "You don't get to threaten our person!"

Sage darted between Dina's feet, tripping her. She went down hard, the gun skittering across the floor.

Lily grabbed it before Dina could recover.

In the bookshop, Albert had managed to fend off the hawk, blood streaming from deep scratches across his face and hands. One eye was swollen shut, the other wild with rage. He raised his gun toward me, his aim unsteady but close enough.

"You're dead," he snarled. "You're all—"

The front door of the bookshop exploded inward.

Sheriff Iris, weapon drawn, Deputy Martinez right behind her.

"Drop it!" Iris shouted. "Now!"

For one terrible moment, I thought Albert might fire anyway. Might take me with him in one final act of spite. His finger tightened on the trigger.

Then his shoulders slumped. The gun clattered to the floor.

"On your knees," Iris commanded. "Hands behind your head."

Albert complied, his cold eyes never leaving my face even through the blood streaming down his forehead. "This isn't over," he said quietly. "The Meridian Group doesn't forget. Doesn't forgive."

"That's enough." Iris kicked his gun away and cuffed him with practiced efficiency. "Albert Crane—or whatever your real name is— you're under arrest for the murder of Grant Granger, attempted murder of Deputy Hank Roberts, breaking and entering, and assault with a deadly weapon. You have the right to remain silent..."

I stopped listening. My legs gave out, and I slid down the counter to sit on the floor, shaking uncontrollably.

It was over.

It was finally over.

The hawk landed on a bookshelf nearby, ruffling its feathers. Blood stained its talons, and several feathers were bent, but it seemed otherwise unharmed. Through it, I could feel Atticus's presence, his relief and exhaustion mixing with my own.

"Thank you," I whispered to the bird. "Tell Atticus thank you."

The hawk tilted its head, regarding me with one bright eye. Then it launched itself back through the shattered skylight and disappeared into the night.

In the back room, I could hear Dina sobbing as Martinez read her rights. The cats were winding around Lily's ankles, triumphant and proud.

"We did it," Rocky announced, his orange fur still puffed with adrenaline. "We fought the bad people and we won!"

"You were so brave," I said, my voice hoarse. "All of you. You were all so brave."

"We couldn't let them hurt you," Poppy said, jumping onto my lap and pressing her head against my chest. "You're ours. We protect what's ours."

Gus approached more slowly, his dignity somewhat restored. "The black and white one fought well," he admitted. "For a human."

"That was the sheriff," I said.

"Ah. That explains the authority in her voice."

Millie crept out from wherever she'd hidden after the initial attack, her blue eyes still huge with fading terror. "Is it over? Are we safe?"

"We're safe," I promised her. "It's over."

Sage bounded over, unable to contain her energy despite everything. "Did you see me? I tripped the bad lady! She fell right over!"

"I saw. You were amazing."

Maeve appeared in the doorway, the silver light fading from the walls as she lowered her arms. She looked exhausted, older than I'd ever seen her, the lines in her face deeper in the returning shadows.

"It's done," she said quietly. "The wards are resealing. But the door..." She looked at the splintered remains of her back entrance, the cold wind pouring through. "It will take time to repair. And the skylight."

"Hank," I said suddenly, my stomach dropping as I remembered Albert's cold words. "Albert said he killed Hank—"

Iris emerged from the bookshop with Albert in custody, her expression grim but with something like relief underneath. "Hank's alive. Martinez found him in the cruiser, conscious and cursing. Took one in the shoulder, but he was wearing his vest. The second shot missed entirely." She shoved Albert forward. "This one was too arrogant to check his work."

Albert's jaw tightened, the first crack in his cold composure.

"Ambulance is on the way," Iris continued. "He's going to make it."

Relief washed through me so strongly I nearly started crying. Hank was alive. Everyone was alive.

Lily helped me to my feet, and I leaned against her, too tired to stand on my own. The cats clustered around us, refusing to let me out of their sight.

And then, at the edge of my awareness, I felt something else. The watching.

It was still there, that ancient presence that had been circling for days. But something was different. The pressure had eased. The testing had stopped. And underneath the usual sense of patient observation, I felt something I hadn't expected.

Relief.

It was relieved that I was okay.

The realization made me shiver in a way that had nothing to do with the cold air pouring through the broken door. Whatever was watching me, whatever had been searching for so long, it cared whether I lived or died. That should have been comforting.

Instead, it raised a thousand new questions I was too exhausted to think about tonight.

Maeve surveyed the damage to her home, her expression weary but practical. "You can't stay here tonight. Not with the door gone and the skylight shattered. It's not safe, and it's certainly not warm."

"My apartment," Lily offered immediately. "It's small, but it's intact. And it's close."

"The cats—" I started.

"Can come too. All of them." Lily squeezed my arm. "I'm not letting you out of my sight tonight. Any of you."

I looked at Maeve. "What about you?"

"I'll stay here. Someone needs to guard what's left of my wards until repairs can be made." She managed a tired smile. "I've weathered worse than a broken door, child. Go. Rest. I'll be fine."

I wanted to argue, but I was too exhausted. And she was right. The cats needed warmth and safety, and right now, Lily's apartment could provide that better than Maeve's damaged sanctuary.

"Tomorrow," I said. "I'll come back tomorrow. Help you clean up."

"Tomorrow," Maeve agreed. "Now go, before you fall over."

We gathered the cats into their carriers, a process made more complicated by their refusal to leave my side. Rocky kept trying to climb back out, insisting he needed to "guard the perimeter." Poppy finally convinced him that guarding me was more important.

The walk to Lily's apartment was short but cold, the winter air biting through my coat. Deputy Martinez escorted us, his hand on his weapon, eyes scanning every shadow. But the streets were quiet. The danger had passed.

For now.

Lily's apartment was small and cluttered with crystals and herbs, but it was warm and whole and safe. The cats explored cautiously at first, then settled into various corners, too tired for their usual territorial investigations.

"The couch pulls out," Lily said, already gathering blankets. "It's not much, but—"

"It's perfect," I said. "Thank you."

Tomorrow would be soon enough for everything else. Tomorrow I would deal with the aftermath, the statements, the repairs. Tomorrow I would think about the watching presence and what it might mean. Tomorrow I would face whatever came next.

Tonight, I just wanted to hold my cats and sleep without fear for the first time in a week.

# Chapter Twenty

Two weeks.

It had taken two weeks for life to feel normal again. Two weeks of repairs and cleaning and slowly putting my café back together. Two weeks of statements and interviews and watching the news cover the arrest of two suspects in the Grant Granger murder case. Two weeks of nightmares that were gradually, mercifully, fading.

But now, on this bright Thursday morning, The Cozy Purrch was open again.

I stood behind the counter, breathing in the familiar smell of fresh coffee and Flo's pastries. The morning light streamed through the new windows. Everything was back in its place. The bookshelves restocked. The cat trees reassembled. The cushions replaced, the dishes restored, the damage erased.

Well. Almost erased. Some scars didn't show on the surface.

"It feels good," Poppy said from her heated bed. "The café feels like itself again."

"It does," I agreed.

The cats had settled back into their routines with remarkable resilience. Gus claimed his high perch, surveying his domain with typical disdain. Rocky bounced from surface to surface, his chaos restored, occasionally stopping to sniff at corners as if checking for intruders. Millie hid behind her fern, peeking out at customers with cautious curiosity. And Sage, no longer quite so much a kitten, had found a sunny spot by the window that she'd claimed as her own.

"We're heroes now," Rocky reminded me for perhaps the hundredth time. "We fought the bad people. We won."

"You did. And I'm very proud of you. All of you."

"Gus bit the accountant lady," Sage added helpfully. "Right on the hand. She screamed."

"I remember."

"She deserved it," Gus said from his perch, with immense dignity. "She pointed a gun at my family."

In the adoption room, three new rescues were settling in. A fluffy orange tabby named Kimchi, already a favorite with the morning crowd. A sleek black cat called Midnight, who had a dignified air that reminded me of Gus. And a tiny calico named Sushi, barely six months old, who had already found a partner in crime.

Through the glass partition, I watched Sushi and Sage tumbling over each other, pouncing on shadows that danced across the floor. They were nearly the same size now, Sage having grown so much in the past few months, and they moved in perfect sync, chasing the same dust mote, batting at the same patch of sunlight.

"They're going to be trouble," Poppy observed.

"The best kind of trouble," I said.

"Kimchi talks too much," Poppy added. "But his heart is good. He'll find a home soon."

"Everyone adjusts at their own pace."

"Some faster than others." She gave me a meaningful look. "Speaking of adjusting. Have you decided yet?"

"Decided what?"

"Don't play coy with me, Alexis. You know exactly what I'm asking."

I did know. I just wasn't ready to answer.

The door chimed, and my first customer of the morning walked in. Not a customer, actually. Hugh Leland, my neighbor, a fresh bandage still visible at his temple but his color good and his smile warm.

"Morning, Alexis," he said, settling onto a stool at the counter. "Coffee, please. Black."

"Hugh! How are you feeling?"

"Head's still a bit tender, but the doctor says I'm healing up nicely." He touched the bandage gingerly. "Six stitches. I'm told I'll have a dashing scar."

"I'm so sorry. For everything. If I hadn't—"

"Don't you dare apologize," he said firmly. "I'm the one who went and stuck my nose where it didn't belong. Heard that racket and thought I'd play hero." He chuckled. "Should've known better at my age."

"You were trying to help."

"And I'd do it again. That's what neighbors are for." He accepted the coffee I poured him, wrapping his hands around the warm mug. "Besides, I hear you caught the people responsible. That's what matters."

"The sheriff caught them. I just... got in the way a lot."

"From what I hear, you did quite a bit more than that." He took a sip of his coffee, eyes twinkling. "Small town. Word travels."

Iris had stopped by earlier in the week to give me an update. Albert—or whatever his real name was—had been transferred to federal custody. The Meridian Group connections meant the FBI was taking over, and he was facing charges that would keep him in prison for the rest of his life. Murder, attempted murder, racketeering, and a dozen other counts I couldn't keep track of.

Dina had turned state's witness in exchange for a reduced sentence. She'd given up everything she knew about the Meridian Group's operations, names and accounts and money trails that would take investigators months to untangle. She'd still serve time, but considerably less than she would have otherwise.

"Justice," Iris had said. "Maybe not perfect justice. But justice."

It would have to be enough.

Hugh finished his coffee, left a generous tip despite my protests, and headed out with a wave and a promise to see me soon. I watched him go, grateful beyond words that he was okay. That everyone was okay.

Well. Almost everyone. Hank was still recovering, his shoulder healing slowly. But he'd stopped by last week, arm in a sling, to tell me he didn't blame me for any of it. "Part of the job," he'd said with a shrug. "Besides, I got to say I took a bullet protecting civilians. Makes for a good story at the bar."

The door chimed again, and Lionel walked in.

He looked the same as always. Strawberry blond hair slightly windswept, green eyes warm behind his glasses. He wore his usual jacket, the one with the patches on the elbows, and carried a book tucked under one arm.

"Morning," he said, approaching the counter with an easy smile. "The usual, please. To go."

"Coming right up."

I made his drink, a Dandelion Root Revival, the herbal tea blend he'd ordered every Friday for as long as I could remember. He didn't hover or make small talk while I worked. Just waited, comfortable in the silence.

"I'm glad you're okay," he said as I handed him the cup. "And that you were able to reopen. The town wasn't the same without this place."

"Thank you. It feels good to be back."

"I can imagine." He tucked the tea into his hand, the book shifting under his arm. I caught the title: something about the history of comic book art. Research for the shop, probably. "See you Friday for game night?"

"I'll be there."

"Good." His smile widened just a fraction. "It wouldn't be the same without you."

He left with a small wave, the door chiming softly behind him. No lingering. No pressure. Just warmth and patience, the way it always was with Lionel.

"I like that one," Poppy said.

"I know you do."

"He smells like paper and contentment. Very calming." She stretched in her heated bed. "The other one smells like anxiety. Always reaching, always wanting. It's exhausting just being near him."

"Poppy..."

"I'm just saying. You asked for our opinions weeks ago. We gave them. You're the one who hasn't listened."

The morning rush picked up after that, saving me from further interrogation. Regulars stopping in for their usuals, tourists discovering the café for the first time, a steady stream of familiar faces and friendly greetings. Esther came by during her planning period with another order for the English department. Flo stopped in to check on me, hugging me tight and reminding me that Sunday dinner was still mandatory. Even Atticus appeared, looking more at peace than I'd ever seen him, ordering a black coffee and settling into a corner table with a sketchbook.

"Maeve says I'm making real progress," he told me when I brought over a refill. "The connection is getting easier to control."

"I'm glad. You're doing great."

"Couldn't have done it without all of you." He hesitated, then added, "Odin says hello, by the way. He's watching from the roof of the hardware store."

"Odin?"

"The hawk." Atticus smiled, a little sheepish. "Maeve said I should name him. Said it would strengthen the bond. Odin seemed to fit. He sees everything."

"Tell Odin I said hello back. And thank him again for saving our lives."

Maeve herself had stopped by yesterday, her home and shop finally repaired. The door had been replaced, the skylight fixed, her wards reinforced and stronger than ever. She'd looked tired but content, and she'd brought me a small bundle of herbs for protection.

"Keep these in the café," she'd said. "Just in case."

I hadn't asked just in case of what. I wasn't sure I wanted to know. I hadn't felt the watching since that night, the ancient presence that had circled and tested and somehow felt relieved when I survived. But I had a feeling it wasn't over yet. Whatever had been searching for me was still out there, patient and waiting.

That was a problem for another day. Maybe another book in my life's strange story.

Around eleven, the door chimed again, and Colton walked in.

He looked good, the way he always did. Put together. Professional. His hazel eyes found me immediately, and he smiled as he approached the counter.

"Hey, you," he said. "I was hoping I'd catch you."

"Hey. What can I get you?"

"Just a latte. For here, if you have time to sit for a minute."

I glanced around the café. The rush had died down. Lily was restocking the pastry case. There was no real reason to say no.

"Sure. Give me a minute."

I made his latte and my own tea, then joined him at a table by the window. He reached across immediately, taking my hand.

"I've been worried about you," he said. "After everything that happened. I wanted to give you space, but..." He squeezed my fingers. "I missed you."

"I'm okay. Really. It's been a lot, but I'm getting through it."

"I know you are. You're strong." His thumb traced circles on the back of my hand. "I was thinking, once things settle down more, maybe we could take a trip somewhere. Get out of town for a weekend. Just the two of us."

It was a nice offer. A thoughtful offer. The kind of thing a caring boyfriend would suggest.

But sitting there, his hand warm on mine, I found myself thinking about Lionel.

Lionel, who never pushed. Who never tried to claim me or plan our future. Who simply showed up, week after week, offering friendship and patience without expectation.

*See you Friday for game night?* That was all he'd asked. All he ever asked.

From her heated bed, Poppy caught my eye. She didn't say anything. She didn't need to.

And suddenly, with a clarity that surprised me, I knew.

"Colton," I said gently, pulling my hand back. "I need to tell you something."

His expression flickered. "That doesn't sound good."

"It's not bad, exactly. It's just..." I took a breath. "You're a good man. You really are. You're kind and attentive and everything anyone could want."

"But?"

"But I don't think we're right for each other. Not in the long run." I met his eyes, forcing myself not to look away. "You deserve someone who's all in. Someone who doesn't have doubts. And I... I have doubts, Colton. I've had them for a while."

He was quiet for a moment, processing. "Is there someone else?"

I thought about lying. About making this easier. But Colton deserved honesty.

"I think there might be," I admitted. "I'm not sure yet. I need time to figure it out. But I know that stringing you along while I figure it out isn't fair to you."

He nodded slowly, something like understanding settling into his features. "It's Lionel, isn't it?"

"I... how did you know?"

"I saw the way he looked at you. At game night. And the way you looked back." He managed a small, sad smile. "I was hoping I was wrong."

"I'm sorry, Colton."

"Don't be. You can't help how you feel." He stood, leaving his untouched latte on the table. "I hope he makes you happy, Alexis. I really do."

"Thank you. For understanding."

He left without another word, the door chiming softly behind him. I sat there for a long moment, staring at my tea, trying to sort through the tangle of emotions in my chest.

"You did the right thing," Poppy said quietly.

"Did I?"

"Yes. He wasn't right for you. Too much grabbing, not enough giving." She jumped down from her bed and padded over, jumping onto the chair Colton had vacated. "The other one gives. He waits. That's what you need."

Then I looked up at Lily.

She was watching me from behind the counter, a knowing smile on her face. Before I could even speak, she said, "Go. I'll watch the shop."

"Lily—"

"Go."

I didn't need to be told a third time.

I was out the door before I could second-guess myself, the cold air hitting my face as I hurried down Main Street. Three doors down. That's all it was. Three doors to The Rebel Rogue.

I pushed open the door, the familiar chime announcing my arrival. The shop was quiet, a few customers browsing the shelves of comics and collectibles. And there, behind the counter, was Lionel.

He looked up when I entered. His green eyes met mine, and something shifted in his expression. Recognition. Hope. A question he was too patient to ask.

He knew. Somehow, he knew.

He came around the counter, moving toward me with purpose. "Alexis?"

I smiled. Nodded.

And then he was there, right in front of me, close enough to touch. His hand came up to cup my face, gentle, questioning.

I answered by closing the distance between us.

The kiss was soft at first, tentative. Then deeper, more certain. Everything I'd been afraid to want, everything I'd been too scared to reach for, finally within my grasp.

When we pulled apart, Lionel was smiling. That quiet, patient smile I'd come to love without even realizing it.

"I was hoping," he said softly. "But I didn't want to assume."

"You never do." I laughed, a little breathless. "That's one of the things I love about you."

His smile widened. "One of them?"

"I'll tell you the others. Eventually."

"I've got time." He took my hand, lacing his fingers through mine. "All the time in the world."

Behind us, the door chimed as a customer entered. The shop needed tending. The café needed me back. Real life was waiting, with all its demands and complications.

But for this one perfect moment, none of that mattered.

I'd found what I was looking for.

And it had been three doors down all along.

**THE END**

**Before you go**: If you loved Claws at the Falls, be sure to visit my website to sign up for my newsletter (if you haven't already) and to stay up to date on new releases and other bookish things.

When signing up, you will receive **either a prequel from my Medium with a Heart series or a recipe that goes along with my Alphabet Soup Series. Your choice!**

Also, check out my other books! You can find links on my website.

www.ejwheltonwrites.com

**Author note:**

Thank you so much for returning to Larkspur Valley and spending more time at The Cozy Purrch. Writing this third installment has been an absolute joy.

This book held a special place in my heart for several reasons, but chief among them was the opportunity to showcase Atticus Monroe. From the moment he appeared as the quiet, steady park ranger who knew the mountain trails better than anyone, I knew there was more to him. Getting to explore his awakening gift and watch him struggle to understand abilities he never asked for felt deeply meaningful. There is something beautiful about characters who discover magic later in life, and Atticus's journey is just beginning.

I also have to admit this book made me emotional to write. Those of you who have been following along since the beginning know that Alexis's heart has been torn between two very different men. Writing that resolution was something I approached with great care. I wanted Alexis to choose not because one man was wrong, but because one was right for her. The moment she walked into The Rebel Rogue, her heart finally certain, might be my favorite scene I have ever written. Love that waits, love that gives space, love that trusts you to find your own way. That felt worth celebrating.

Thank you for walking these snowy mountain trails with Alexis and her feline family. There are more mysteries waiting in Larkspur Valley, and I cannot wait to share them with you.

Until next time, may your coffee be warm and your cats be close.

www.ejwheltonwrites.com